Bertha Jane Laffan

**The Peyton Romance**

Part 2

Bertha Jane Laffan

**The Peyton Romance**
*Part 2*

ISBN/EAN: 9783337052263

Printed in Europe, USA, Canada, Australia, Japan

Cover: Foto ©Andreas Hilbeck / pixelio.de

More available books at **www.hansebooks.com**

BY

# Mrs. LEITH ADAMS

(Mrs. R. S. DE COURCY LAFFAN)

AUTHOR OF

"BONNIE KATE," "A GARRISON ROMANCE," "LOUIS DRAYCOTT," ETC.

*IN THREE VOLUMES*

VOL. II.

## LONDON

KEGAN PAUL, TRENCH, TRÜBNER, & CO. L$^{TD}$

PATERNOSTER HOUSE, CHARING CROSS ROAD

1892

# CONTENTS.

## VOLUME II.

# THE PEYTON ROMANCE.

## CHAPTER I.

### "THE ROCK."

THE tall white lilies were all ablow, pure and stately in the radiant light; not just a few lilies here and there, as you see in English gardens, but hundreds, lifting in serried rows their pure chalices to the purple sky, with golden stamens gleaming bright; flowering shrubs, trees drooping earthward because their sweet load of blossoms weighed them down; roses—oh, such roses!—white and red and palest pink; some cream, some crimson, that were black as you looked into their folded hearts, and made the senses reel with their perfume: while jasmine and violets

blossomed everywhere. Sunshine, not yet
grown hot enough to scorch and blind, but
warm and bright, everywhere, too, scattering
the blue, blue waters into diamonds that
flashed and scintillated, bathing the mighty
rock—the towering fortress of Gibraltar—
in such a flood of light that it shone even
as the walls of some marble palace of the
gods, while at its feet, that were bathed in
the " calm translucent wave " of the purple
Mediterranean, clustered fishing-smacks with
ruddy sails, yachts, white-winged little plea-
sure-boats with gay-striped awnings, and,
some little way out, stately ships, like mighty
birds at rest with folded pinions on the
placid breast of the sunbright sea.

In the fissures that here and there varied
the surface of the rock nestled groups of
acacias, their amber blossoms drooping downwards like the loose tresses of a woman's
golden hair ; orange-trees not yet in blossom,
but pricked with silver buds ; and figs, their
leaves of luscious green, their fruit as yet
but groups of tiny buttons, like clustered

emeralds. At the western side of the great rock the town of Gibraltar itself was seen, looking, when seen from a distance, like a toy village that is put away in a box at night — so bright, so clean, so gay, with awning and draped balcony, with villas surrounded by verandahs festooned with flowering creepers, with gay shops, with soldiers white helmeted, with horses caracoling in the streets, and ladies fair here, there, and everywhere. Spanish donnas, too, might be seen, with eyes like jewels, gleaming dark and bright, and raven tresses snooded with the famed mantilla, and quaint, picturesque figures, priests, friars, mule-drivers, boatmen, natives of the place, looking like the pictures you may see on the lids of fancy boxes, and all smoking the universal cigar, even the poorest, while tiny dark-eyed children, dressed as you might expect to see the children of the people on the fancy boxes, crowded in every shady corner, and ate fruit, both ripe and unripe, with an absolute disregard of consequences.

I remember seeing a tiny child seated at the top of the harbour steps in Malta, clasping in its arms a melon almost as big as itself. To my horror, as I watched, the little creature overbalanced itself, and rolled down the first flight—still, however, clasping the melon close. Child and melon made a rapid descent, but never once did the little olive-tinted hands let go their prize, and when I rushed down, expecting to see the little one in bits, lo! there it was, seated serenely smiling, with a bump on its forehead and a bloody nose, but otherwise calm and unmoved, patting the fat, golden melon, and asking in Maltese *patois* for an "ever so little knife to cut the plenty pretty, plenty big melon."

There is something bewilderingly delightful in the plenitude and profusion of fruit and flowers in such places as Malta and Gibraltar, and a charm unspeakable in the fitful sound of music, that is seldom absent, the tinkle of a mandoline, the trill of a zither, or the sparkling rhythm of a military band. Life seems to sit more easily on people in

such lands, care to press less heavily; of
poverty — the squalid, grinding, unlovely
poverty such as is to be found in our awful
rookeries and nameless wynds and alleys—
there is none. A beggar begs, and manages
to make himself picturesque over it somehow
in spite of rags and dirt; but no one ever
starves, since all can live on figs and bread,
with a sprinkling of olive-oil and oranges
hot from the kisses of the sun.

A merry, happy, thoughtless kind of life is
that in those fair garrisons—the gay daughters
of the old mother-country. Pestilence comes
sometimes, and fever-blasts and tropic storms,
but these pass and are forgotten, and the
orange-trees blossom, and the band plays,
and the lilies lift their faces, passion-pale, to
the silvery moon; the blue, dark water is
smitten by the pulsing oars, and the boat-
man once more sings as he sways.

Nature is so kind that she cannot frown
long; so gay and bright that when she weeps
the sunshine quickly turns her tears to jewels
bright as stars.

What would Master Straw have said if he could have seen Danny Spool strolling down the gay, bright streets of "Gib," a natty little cane in his hand, his cap miraculously balanced on a single hair, and looking as if the whole garrison, fortress included, belonged to him? What would Master Straw have said if he could have seen Danny performing as a step-dancer at the soldiers' social evenings, or playing on a penny-whistle with such excruciating skill and ingenuity that the audience fairly rose at him, and roared at him, and even the Colonel commanding—a mighty and awe-inspiring personage—faintly beat the palms of his gracious hands together? After this Danny became, as it were, a kind of glorified drummer-boy, and other drummer-boys asked him " if he'd shwallowed his cane by any accident, that he carried his blessed self so stiff an' tall, and niver once looked at the ground he walked on at all, at all?" with other pleasantries of the same description.

It may be gathered that the 97th were

having gay times enough at the Rock, and no man in the fine old regiment was gayer or happier than Ensign Cyril Peyton.

"It's wonderful," he said to his friend Percy Dighton, "how much nearer home one feels here, isn't it, old fellow, though the sea rolls between us still, and leave isn't scattered too plentifully among us by any means, is it?"

"Is there some strong and fair attraction in the old country, eh, Peyton?" said the other, laughing.

"Nothing stronger than a longing to see my mother again," said Cyril. "I've often felt, when we were out there," pointing to the sky-line, by way of indicating India's coral strand, "like a schoolboy at the beginning of term, and now I feel like a schoolboy with the holidays well in view; I do indeed. Even one's home letters seem to come from somewhere quite close at hand—it's all quite different—quite, quite different. Do you know, I have never forgotten just the look of my mother's face as I caught the last glimpse of her. She was leaning a little forward, her hands clasped, her face white as a statue, and her eyes seemed to burn into me as I looked; then she threw up her arms, and sank upon her knees; I could see her bowed head—I can see it now."

The young soldier to whom he spoke looked very grave and thoughtful, and just a little shamefaced.

"I know now, Peyton," he said presently, "why you have always been, in many ways, so different to the rest of us—how it is you have helped other fellows."

"Have I helped other fellows?" said young Peyton, turning his bright face to his companion. "It must have been without knowing it, then, except, of course, when poor old Fullerton—— But there! any fellow would have helped Fullerton."

"We all had the heart to, of course, but we're such extravagant dogs; it's hard to stump up at a day's notice to the tune of—well—well, I forget what it was, but enough to break most of us, or drive us into the clutches of the sons of Israel."

" There again," said Ensign Peyton, " I
have to thank my mother for a good deal;
she keeps the governor up to the mark, and
I've got no extravagant tastes, except Caliph.
I almost thought, though, Caliph would have
to go that time. It was rather a tight place,"
he went on, with a wince.

" Very," said the other laconically; " Shall
you ever forget Fullerton in Curzon's room,
blubbering like a baby, with his head on the
table, and asking if anybody would be kind
enough to shoot him ?"

" Poor little devil !" said Peyton, " he was
more sinned against than sinning—got desperate, you know, and then——"

" Just so ! I think I see the Badger " (regimental sobriquet for one Walsingham, captain
No. 10 Company) " stepping gingerly, as if
on eggs, and craftily removing poor Fullerton's
razors, making the most excruciating grimaces
at us the while, by way of caution."

" That's the Badger all over," said Peyton,
with a ring of boyish laughter; " and then he
brought me two dollar pieces and an English

sixpence, and, 'Pon my life,' says he, 'it's all I have, Peyton, and poor Fullerton's welcome to it, every cent. There's the locket, too, with the likeness of the last girl I was engaged to—could anything be done with that?'"

The two men were strolling up and down the enclosure opposite the officers' quarters. They had come off parade, and with tunics unbuttoned, and helmets pushed back almost on to the napes of their necks, were doing a leisurely sort of "sentry-go," enjoying the luxury of a smoke.

At intervals were set great tubs, each having its own special orange-tree, bristling with white and snowy buds, and clambering up the face of the quarters was a grand datura, just now only a mass of velvety leaves, but shortly to show the big pale trumpet-flowers of its kind, and give luscious and unstinted store of perfume.

On the steps of the high arched door lounged a group of men—also "loose from parade," as the saying goes; also *degagé* in

their style of attire; also sending forth pale
blue rings of smoke into the clear air.

"This isn't half a bad place," said Peyton,
leaning his arms on the balustrade, and looking out towards the blue and sparkling sea,
with its flotilla of small and great ships.

"It's glorious," replied Dighton, "and as
for an odd scorpion or two, what's that after
the chance of a cobra in your boot, or coiled
up in your bath ready to help you to begin
the day well? I shall write and tell my people
I look upon Gib as only second to what the
Garden of Eden might have been. By Jove,
Peyton! I've seen more pretty girls in one
day here than I saw in a year in what my
man calls the 'Hindies.'"

"Be sure and tell your people that," laughed
a man who had just lounged across from the
doorway; "they'll be awfully pleased, you
know, to hear that—one's people always
are."

"They always think evewy girl wants to
mawwy one, don't you know," put in a pecu-
liarly meek-looking youngster with a long

pale nose, retreating chin, and most aggressive moustache.

"You can tell them a thing worth two of that, can't you, Wobbler?" said Dighton with cruelty, for it was notorious that the said Wobbler (real name Anstruther) had been twice rejected by the aspiring daughter of a Civil Service man, who only "drew on" ensigns, lieutenants, and such-like small deer, to play them off against big game.

"Vewy unkind cut that, I'm shaw," said Wobbler, screwing his glass into his eye, and trying to look the offender down. "Why should you wemind a fellah of his misfortunes?"

> "Oh, why did she flatter my boyish pride,
> To leave me lonely now?"

trolled Captain Gerald Gildea, an Irishman with soft blue eyes and a sonsie smile. "That's about it, isn't it, Wobbler my boy? Sure and it was a shame to trifle with your young affections that way."

The Wobbler wobbled off; most of the

other men strolled quietly away, and soon
Cyril Peyton was left in sole possession of
the enclosure.

He was not a man given to softness and
reverie by any means, but to-day, for some
reason or other, his usual vivacity and spring
forsook him. How beautiful looked the world
of sea and land lying at his feet! The
scene was all dancing sunshine, green leaves,
and sparkling music—music so softened by
distance that it seemed as natural an out-
come of the day as might the lilting of birds
in the groves of orange, fig, and acacia that
looked like green mists against the marble
grey of the Rock.

A band was practising on board a great
ship that was anchored far out in the blue
water. The tune it played was one his
mother used to sing (for those two had been
wont to sing to each other sometimes when
Sir Marmaduke was away), and the ring of
it brought back to Cyril's mind the high
mullioned window, the piano just where
the light fell full upon it, the deft white

hands upon the keys, the dear face up-
lifted, the soft rich voice—

> " Su passaggieri, venite via !
>     Santa Lucia, Santa Lucia ! "

Ah ! what memories will cling round a melody
that rises from the dear dead past, like the
faint, sweet perfume from a withered flower !

Private Dorrington (now promoted to
" privilege," and revelling in all the glory
of a servant's mufti) passing through to the
quarters, after getting himself out of parade
uniform, took a glance at his master, and
thought to himself—

" He's thinking of the old home and them
as is far away, is Master Cyril."

It almost seemed a breach of military
discipline even to think the name that had
been so familiar in the olden days, and the
man's hand rose to his cap with a jerk as
Ensign Peyton turned and faced him.

But for all that, Private Dorrington looked
like a thing cut out of wood, and had about
as much expression in his face as any one

of the figure-heads of the vessels anchored below; he was sure, at that moment, that his ideas had, to use his own expression, " run straight," and that " Master Cyril," had been thinking of her Ladyship and the Old Hall, and, maybe, of the dog that used to follow at his heels. There was something in his master's face that seemed to tell Dorrington all this, and a much stronger impression was made upon his mind than the occasion appeared to warrant.

"See that Caliph is ready in an hour's time."

" Yessir."

The master had given his order; the wooden figure had answered like an automaton.

Then young Peyton moved across towards his rooms, but not without a backward glance at the quiet bay and the ships that slept in the sunshine.

> " Su passaggieri, venite via !
> Santa Lucia, Santa Lucia ! "

rang out softly on the sunbright air, and

still Cyril lingered, one foot on the step, his head turned over his shoulder. Is it so, that about us and around us are such strange mysterious influences, that the coming events in our lives cast their shadows across our pathway, and, conscious of a premonition, we know not why or of what—we look with lingering eyes upon scenes that are never again seen through the same placid medium ?

It was not often that Cyril Peyton set forth on a ride alone. Often he made one of a gay cavalcade of sprightly amazons and attendant cavaliers, reining in spirited steeds, and sitting their saddles as though to the manner born. Often, a friend on this side and a friend on that, he would make for the famed cork-woods, and there delight in the "fragrant aromatic shade," the dappled light falling through the weft of leaves, the green boughs showing bravely against the sunshine.

To-day he craved no company but his own. His mind had flown homeward to the York-

shire dales. As Caliph, in whose silken sides
you might see yourself, and whose proud
feet seemed to spurn the earth they trod,
paced slowly on, Cyril caught sight of Drummer Danny, his cap miraculously balanced
as usual, his droll hatchet-shaped face all
lighted up with pleasure at the sight of
Caliph and his rider. The little figure, looking like a toy-soldier, drew up stiffly by the
side of the white hard road, the hand flew
to the jaunty cap.

What a miniature warrior it looked—what
an elf in scarlet, to be sure!

A companion (also apparently a toy-soldier)
was with it, and the two whispered and
grimaced after the horse and rider had passed.

"I knowed 'im, you know, when I was a
blooming civilian," said Danny, waving a
scarlet arm to indicate the officer who had
just passed. "He comed from where I comed
from; we each comed from where the other
comed from; I follered on to him here, 'cos
the place was so kinder lonesome wi'out 'im.
I come as a stowaway, you know, and no

one knowed.  I thought nothin' of mysel', no
more than if I was an old portmantel, only so
as I could come along.  Private Dorrington,
him as is batman to him, he thought nothin'
of hisself either, only so as he could come
along.  I'm telling you these things, my boy,
'cos you've just jined, and don't know nothin'
about anythink, you don't."

This last remark was uttered with a whisk
of the smart little cane Danny carried, and an
indescribable air of patronage—an air as of one
who should say, "I'm a man of the world,
you see ; if you're led by me, you can't go far
wrong, and that's all about it."

Danny was very happy.  He was taking
the newly-joined drummer-boy about, and
telling him frightful and altogether men-
dacious stories of men and things.  But all
he said about Ensign Peyton was Gospel
truth, and the newly-fledged drummer felt it
was so, and watched the rider with admiring
eyes until a turn in the road hid him from
sight.

"Shure, an' he's the broth o' the boy

entoirely," said the new drummer, "an' that's thrue for ye."

Transfixed, as it were, by the audacity that thus dare take "Maister Cyril's" name on his lip so freely, Danny was on him in a moment —that is, figuratively. Outwardly his demeanour was unchanged. He held his head as upright as a dart, only the blue eyes glaring round the corner, and he swished his cane.

"The sergeant says we're to keep select and straight out in the streets, and do nothing to disgrace the regiment, so I'll have to keep the drubbing I've got for you till we're in the barrack-yard," said Danny. "I'll larn you to speak familler o' them as you ain't fit to black the blessed boots of."

Meanwhile, unconscious of the comments made upon him behind his back, Cyril rode joyously onward—rode on—rode on—to meet the fate that lay in wait for him.

He was soon some miles away from the fort, and only here and there were scattered little houses, closely walled, with just the tips of fig or orange tree peeping above the high copings.

Caliph had dropped into a walk, a dainty sort of high-stepping proceeding quite peculiar to himself; the reins hung loosely. Cyril's thoughts still clung about and centred in the "auld house at home," and he remembered gladly that that very day was mail day, and letters would come to him—letters faintly perfumed with the scent of sandalwood, and suggesting his mother's hand and the delicate cobweb-like laces that hung about her white, blue-veined wrist.

Cyril was brought back to the present with a jerk.

Caliph had set his front legs stiffly, and given a snort.

Something had come "betwixt the wind and his nobility." They had just turned a rather sharp corner, and there by the road-side was a little black heap, out of which looked an elf-like face, almost monkey-like indeed in its withered, wizened cheeks and prominent working lips—in a word, he saw the puckered face of an old Spanish crone, or rather a crone of the sort of half-breed that is called a "Rock scorpion" by playful Britishers. These people are often, nay, generally, beautiful in youth, but become obese in middle age, and wither, like long-kept apples, in old age.

Cries of fear and distress, inarticulate—at all events to Cyril Peyton—came from the woman's skinny lips, and one of her tawny hands was working in mid-air, as if to signal to the heavens for succour.

In a moment Cyril was out of his saddle, and Caliph, unwilling, sullen, shivering in his satin skin, tied to a sapling olive, and bid to "stand."

Cyril had by this time grasped the fact that the dark heap on the white dusty roadside was composed of two persons, and that the slender form of a girl lay across, and supported by, the older woman's knee.

A moment more, and he realised also that he was gazing on the most perfectly beautiful face he had ever yet seen—a face like a dream, like a picture, anything you will, yet without life.

For the eyes were closed, and the long lashes—he had not thought a woman *could* have such long lashes—lay upon the satin cheeks. The delicate flower-like lips were open, "like the cleft in a pomegranate," and showed within the gleam of little pearl-like teeth. The brow was low and broad, and the lovely tendrils of black silken hair clustered about it, rippling down behind the small ears and about the slender column of the throat. He saw and noted all this in a flash, for the girl's mantilla had fallen off, and one small hand lay prone among the dust. Meanwhile the crone chattered like a magpie, and gesticulated and moved like a witch; and Cyril, who had caught up some Spanish *patois* since he came to the Rock, recognised the word that meant "death," interspersed with little shrieks and appeals to saints male and female, saints big and saints little, and "*Ahimés*" enough to furnish forth a first-class "keening."

He lifted the little hand from the dust,
bent over the beautiful, still face, and then,
in voluble and vigorous English, began to
assure the crone that the lady was not dead
by any means, but had evidently fainted
from some cause or other to him unknown.
It is no use asking how it came about that
the ancient dame understood what the English signor meant. Suffice it to say she did.
They are quick as lightning and sharp as
needles, these old Southern women, and can
say as much with their hands as a dozen
Englishwomen with their tongues, in the
same given space of time. Cyril quickly
understood that the two women—girl and
duenna—had been to church, it being a *festa,*
and, here in this place, close to home (for
which might the blessed saints—here she
crossed herself in a frenzy—be thanked), the
young lady had slipped on a round big stone
(here the crone cursed the stone, spitting out
her words like a cat), had fallen dead, dead
with the tortures of her pains, and the old
woman prayed to her many saints, one of

which had put it into the heart of the English
signor to come that way on his beautiful
*animalito*—and so on, chatter, chatter, chatter,
till Cyril's brain fairly reeled, and he be-
thought him that the best way of all was
to take the law into his own hands—in other
words, to lift the slight girlish form in his
strong and willing arms, and bear her in
the direction of a small low door in a grey
stone wall, the crone having indicated that
safety and succour lay within that barrier.

The old woman, at the sight of this sum-
mary proceeding, began running backwards
and forwards like a mad thing, laughing
and crying and pulling at a slim chain with
an iron tag at the end that hung beside the
door.

At last the portal was reached, and a bent
old man—apparently the masculine counter-
part of the crone—stood holding the door
widely open, and listening in a dazed pur-
blind condition to the torrent of mingled
lamentation, description, and exultation poured
forth by his ancient spouse.

How strangely surprising and pretty are
the glimpses seen through the doors of those
foreign homes!  The blank, chill walls, the
shabby garden-door, how little either pre-
pares you for the blossom-laden oleander,
the little fountain in the square flagged
court, the trellised pathway with its roof of
vine-leaves, and the windows set open amid
a tangle of acacia, roses, and tall climbing
heliotrope with stems as thick as your wrist!

You catch a glimpse of such a charming
interior as this, looking like a sunny bit done
by Macquoid, and then clap-to goes the door,
and nothing is to be seen save the square
ugly wall and the gruesome door of sun-
blistered paint.

Through the midst of oleander, acacia, and
orange-bloom Cyril bore his light burden—
bore the girl tenderly, with the tenderness
that only perfect strength can know, and yet,
even so, was conscious of a moan passing her
lips that paled and shook, and of a pucker of
pain between the finely pencilled brows.

Up three shallow steps and into a sort of

vestibule, preceded by the crone, who never once ceased chattering, went the sad little procession, and there upon some muslin cushions on a wide low couch, according to the old woman's vociferous directions, Cyril laid the still unconscious girl. What a pang of regret chilled his heart as he took his arms from about her, and saw the gracious head that had but now rested on his shoulder sink back upon the faded embroidered pillows !

For a moment he was left alone with her, the crone apparently being engaged in driving forth the old man on some urgent errand with all the force and determination that it may be supposed the armed angels employed in the driving forth of our apocryphal first parents from Eden. It was only, however, the old woman's violent way of doing things that gave this impression. In reality she was only urging her husband to go quickly in search of the native doctor, and the shove that she gave him before shutting the door almost upon him, were only the signs of an amiable anxiety on behalf of her master's niece, la Signorita Juanita Maria Delano.

We have said that Cyril was left alone a moment with the unconscious girl. His youth must plead for him in the fact that he made use of that moment to press one little olive-tinted hand to his audacious lips ; and next, gaining courage as he went on, to touch, with infinite reverence and gentleness, it is true, but yet caressingly, the straying tendrils of the raven locks upon Juanita's brow. She had a name, too, as well as a place in his heart ; for had not the old crone, weeping and wailing, called upon her over and over again as " Signorita—Signorita Juanita mia ? "

Any one looking into that shadow-pied chamber, musical with the drip, drip, drip of the little fountain, and the soft piping cry of some tiny fly-catchers, that flitted about upon the floor darting here and there with flutter of wing and tail and flashes of white breast—any one looking at the two—the maiden and the young man beside her—

—would naturally have thought of the legend of the Sleeping Princess, and been ready to say, "The prince has come at last to wake her with a kiss."

It was not quite a kiss, certainly, but a touch can, at times, say almost as much.

Anyway, Juanita's great dark eyes opened slowly, looked gravely like those of a wondering child into the face that bent above her—the face of Cyril Peyton, whom to look on was to love, and a little dawning smile curved the corners of her mouth.

For a while—a very little while—just, perhaps, while you could count ten—they were motionless, these two, each looking at the other.

In each face was the same look—a look that is like no other; a look that seems to say, "I have been waiting for you, and now —I have found you."

Then in rushed old Maritana, and the spell was broken, the exquisite moment was over. The old woman gave a cry at seeing the girl's eyes open, and Cyril straightened himself, and with arms folded—indubitably an Englishman again in attitude and calmness of demeanour — listened to such a torrent of words, sobs, sighs, ejaculations, witnessed such a succession of signs, contortions, posturings, and frantic gestures as the venerable Maritana considered needful to the telling her young mistress the story of their mutual adventures, and giving a full and fitting explanation of the strange signor's presence in their midst.

Gradually the faint rich colour rose beneath the olive skin, the girl's lips grew crimson, and her eyes flashed. Cyril felt dazed and blinded by the radiance of her beauty. It was like watching a lovely statue come to life; he felt like a second Pygmalion, for if he had not made the statue, surely he had found it, and now it lived, it moved, it breathed before him! He trembled as at last the girl spoke—oh heaven—in what a voice! So soft, so low, that most excellent gift in woman, so thrilled through and through with a tremulous gratitude and joy!

Slowly very slowly, like the first uncertain halting steps of a child that has never walked before, fell the words of a strange and unfamiliar language from the lips that his eyes devoured.

"Some Engleesh I speak. I can say, tank you many times tank you, for to be to me so much kind . . . signor."

It would have taken a very crudite and complete knowledge of the English language to have followed the speech which our foolish boyish Cyril made in reply; and Juanita shook her shapely head, and made pretty bewildered gestures with her hands; but she understood the spirit of it all, and thrilled and trembled under the torrent of the young English milord's eloquence. Indeed, she moved, or tried to move, her injured foot, gave a smothered cry of agony, and sank back once more upon the pillows, almost fainting.

Maritana, at this, signed to Cyril that she feared the lady's ankle was broken—so—and made him understand that the best thing he could do was to go.

Which he did, taking no farewell in speech, but yet looking such a lingering adieu as Romeo may have done when parting from his Capulet.

Once having got the stranger outside, Maritana was prompt in clapping-to the door.

And there stood Cyril, out in the barren dusty road, with the bare grey walls staring at him, saying to himself that surely, surely it must be all a dream, and he the creature of some fond and foolish fancy.

But there was Caliph, tethered to the olive-tree, tossing his velvet-soft nose in the air in contempt at the ignominy of his own position and his master's insane behaviour.

Cyril was in the saddle in a trice, and then, looking up, saw Captain Gildea trotting up the road from the fort on his grey steed Cobnut.

" Hullo ! Why, Peyton ! " cried the young fellow, his soft Irish eyes agleam, a laugh on his lips. But at sight of the other he grew grave. " Is anything the matter, old fellow ?

Have you found the sun a bit too hot?
Wasn't it odd? I fancied you came out of
that shabby old door there—that one in the
grey wall. I did, 'pon honour."

"Did you?" replied Cyril.

And then Gildea saw, in one moment, that
the thing was true, but that Peyton wished
to keep silence.

"Hang it," he thought to himself, as the
two paced on side by side, "other fellows go
in for that sort of thing, and it's natural
enough, but—damn it, it isn't like Peyton!"
and he gave the grey a cut that made that
astonished animal swerve right across the road.
Cyril made no comment. He rode on as one
dazed and dreaming. "Anyway, he's hard
hit," thought Gildea, glancing at the handsome but now pallid face.

"The mail's in," he said at last, "and
you're in the 'Gazette'—Lieutenant Peyton."

"Oh, I've got my step, have I?" said
Cyril carelessly.

Everything in the world seemed so small
and dwarfed beside the thought of Juanita!

# CHAPTER II.

## "I HAVE NO ONE—NO ONE BUT YOU!"

A LINED and wizened face, which, when the man smiled, puckered up into little creases about the eyes, dark and wicked, that watched the world from narrowed lids; a bent heavy back, weak legs, and hands yellow as wax, with long nails, and a way of working one in the other, as though for ever busy transacting ghostly business and formulating schemes— such was Pedro Montalba, well known to the inhabitants of the Rock, English and native; much cultivated, too, by both, in consequence of the delicious cigars sold by him, and the kindly nature of his heart, which led him to do certain kindnesses, " the half in cigars, the rest"—a shrug, a pair of yellow hands up-lifted palms uppermost, expressed the rest

Which " rest " was ofttimes a sore burden

strapped tight on to the shoulders of the young subaltern; for Pedro's rate of interest was unrighteous and horrible; but he was, as said one of his many clients, "a most convenient beast."

His shop was in a shaded nook in a sort of alcove, and herein he seemed to live as a soldier-crab lives in his shell, stretching out his claws to gather in prey, and glaring at the world with small beady eyes.

Nothing could exceed the drollery of Pedro's appearance, with a huge manilla between his glittering white teeth, a small Turkish fez on the back of his bullet-head, and his face ever wrinkled into a thousand tiny creases by a series of marvellous smiles, making a series of bows to passers-by.

" Goot day, sare. *Ahime!* de zun he come mooch strong by de now. Cigar fer you, sare? Cigar, milor? Some splendide joost come. You step in, you sit in my plenty shmall divan, you smoke him. 'Ah, *si, si,*' you say, 'dat is goot. Pedro is goot; my friend Pedro is a goot man.'"

How many heedless feet, stepping into that "small divan," had learnt its secrets all too well—had found present ease and a delightful plenty, to be paid for in the not far distant future in coin called "interest," wrung from the unwilling victim as the teeth were drawn from the bleeding jaws of the Jews in olden times? Pedro might be a "goot man," but if so, his looks belied him; he might be "a convenient beast," as said the needy subaltern, but assuredly he was a dangerous one.

Whether or not he had spies in his employ, no one knew, but his knowledge of every one's affairs was marvellous. You could tell Pedro nothing that he did not know already. He could inform you on subjects which you would have supposed to be entirely out of his beat and ken.

When some youngster who chanced to be next of kin to a wealthy English "milor" arrived in the garrison, Pedro bowed more obsequiously, smiled more greasily, rubbed his hands more persistently than before. His

best goods (and it may be said that he had
one or two brands that none in the known
world could beat) were laid out, sampled,
smoked, purchased, and in nine cases out of
ten nothing more came of the transaction.
Pedro cooled off in his attentions and devo-
tions to the scion of a wealthy house, and
with delicately lifted brows and hands would
cunningly cheapen that young man who was
so ruinously prudent, even going so far, in
one or two cases, as to say, "He is what you
say in Engleesh, one prigue. Pedro loffs not
the Engleesh prigue; he loffs the pleasantness
of the youth that is gay, full of what you
call ze spirits of ze wine, ze spirits of ze fire,
ze lof of ze life."

His listeners would look at each other with
laughing eyes the while, and say, "Pedro,
you are a good man."

"A—h!" would Pedro reply, with an ineffable shrug of the round shoulders, and
an altogether inimitable smirk, "I am ze
best as they make them, but I am too kine.
I have ze heart too beeg, too tender.  I

lose my own a'vantage in ze battle of ze life."

"You can't find it in your heart to put it on, eh, Pedro?" would some saucy boy, fresh from school, put in, intending to be immensely smart.

Then Pedro's face would grow suddenly blank with the absolute know-nothing of a puzzled child.

"Poot it on," he would say; "I can-not know dis word; it is perhaps one of your what you call ee-dee-ums—sings which only ze Engleesh can know. Go long! you make ze gr-reat fun of poor Pedro."

There had not been lacking one or two ugly episodes in Pedro's life, but he had always escaped as by the skin of his teeth.

When poor young Cheriton, of the 183rd, was found with a gash across his throat; when his chosen friend and comrade, bending over him, wept like a woman, and the sturdy surgeon-major of the regiment was as near as possible following suit, to see the boy whom, in spite of his heedless ways, all had loved

so dearly, lying there in such sad case, there
had not been wanting whispers of the name
of Pedro Montalba.  Some said the fish had
been played, and the line let out, and then
tightened suddenly, and the victim landed,
only, however, to escape by a surer way ; but
nothing was ever proved, and of what avail
are mere insinuations ?

For a while men fought shy of the cigar
divan, but as the years passed on the grudge
was forgotten.  Regiments came and regiments went, and the legend died out.

Perhaps the sudden and awful termination
of his tactics in the case of poor Cheriton
made Pedro more cautious.  Certain it is
he grew more subtle, went about his work
more craftily, and refrained—let us hope—
from exacting more than a hundred per cent.
and half the original sum in cigars.  By these
moderate returns he managed to secure a
modest little income, owned a villa at some
distance from the town, where he occasionally
went to spend a Sunday or enjoy a *festa*,
and where, so rumour had it, dwelt a niece

of surpassing beauty and spotless virtue, a
jewel upon whom it was given to no man to
gaze. Pedro was also reported to be ambitious,
and to harbour ideas of one day securing a
grandee of Spain for this paragon.

These things were hinted at, talked over,
speculated about, amongst the youngsters of
the garrison; but Captain Gildea noticed
that Cyril Peyton kept silence, joining in
no speculation, helping on no surmise. Not
only so, but he marked his comrade's many
absences, his *distrait* manner, his dreamy
smile, and marvelled if again and yet again
the sun-blistered door in the dull grey wall
had opened to admit the "English señor"—
if, in a word, Peyton was becoming hopelessly
entangled. Of the nature of the entangle-
ment, if such existed, Gildea could form no
opinion. On the one hand, he could not
bring himself to imagine anything dishonour-
able, anything like "some other fellows"
might do, and think but little of it; and,
on the other hand, for Cyril Peyton, the
scion of an ancient house, to marry a woman

nearly related to that rascally, oily old usurer
seemed impossible !

Why, the chief would go frantic if any
one suggested the possibility of such a catas-
trophe happening in his regiment; and Sir
Marmaduke and Lady Peyton, what would
their feelings be on the matter ? With the
loyalty that seems a natural product of regimental life, Gildea kept what is called "a
quiet tongue in his head." If he had seen
what he was not meant to see, then the
knowledge so acquired had in his code no
existence. Still he could not forget Peyton's
face that day when they met at the place
where the narrow road turned off from the
main way, and the little high-walled villa
nestled in a corner by itself.

Meanwhile Cyril was leading an enchanted
life. The freshness which he had preserved
in so remarkable a degree made his love for
Juanita a very different thing from the love
a jaded man of the world would have had
to bestow upon a woman removed, as she
undoubtedly was, from the sphere of his own

life and surroundings. In this indeed lay,
for Cyril, her greatest charm. He had seen
enough of certain gay and flaunting ladies of
the Indian station; had amused himself, but
never lost even the smallest corner of his
light and merry heart. He had made friends,
many and true, among the wives of his
brother officers, and endeared himself to
them by his kindly pleasant ways, and his
interest in the little ones who grew so pale
under the hot Indian sun, and looked upon
"Mr. Peyton" as quite a playfellow, and
ever a welcome friend. Indeed, there never
was a creature who found himself so univer-
sally made welcome wherever he went as
Lady Peyton's younger son; and when he
was ill, the first and only time the fever-
fiend got him by the throat, did not Major
and Mrs. Kershaw take him into their
bungalow, and nurse him as if he had
been their own younger brother? Did not
the Colonel's wife, that most stately and
chilly of mortals, drive down every day
to ask how he was, and insist upon taking

him out in her own carriage on the occasion of his first appearance in public as a
convalescent ?

Said Mrs. Kershaw to her Major, with the
tears standing in her kind eyes, when Cyril
was thus laid low—

"I can never, never forget, Hubert, how he
used to sit by little Alice and amuse her
by the hour, and how she used to smile to
see him coming, even when she was too weak
to speak. Oh, I hope—I hope he will pull
through; I pray—I pray that he may!"

Now little Alice slept beneath the palm-
trees, where a small white headstone set
forth that the "dear child" of Major and
Mrs. Kershaw, of the 97th, lay there sleeping her last sleep, "aged three and a half
years."

Lady Peyton knew but little of this illness
of Cyril's.

"Don't any one write and worry my
mother; she could not bear it," he had said,
holding Mrs. Kershaw's hand in his, and
looking up into her face with tired beseech-

ing eyes; and, as he soon took a turn for the better—having youth and strength and a clean and temperate life on his side—Lady Peyton was not "worried;" but she knew enough to set the name of Mary Kershaw in her prayers, and to be grateful to the God who had raised up such true friends for her darling in that far and distant land whither he had gone.

All this, to any one who knows the life of a regiment, will show to a turn the sort of fellow Cyril Peyton was, and what freshness of unjaded passion he brought as an offering to the fairy princess of the little grey-walled house, with its inner garden of verdure and blossom. To say that he had any deliberate plans at this time of his life would be untrue. He never sat down and said to himself in cold blood—

"I will marry this girl, foreigner and Roman Catholic as she is, and let things take their course with my people."

Perhaps, if any temptation to such a train of thought had come about, his mind would

have glanced off from it, as a ball rebounds
from an obstacle, struck with the realisation
of what Sir Marmaduke's horror would be
at such an alliance, what his mother's suffering, his brother's estrangement.

Anyhow, he left all these gloomy thoughts
in the shadow that best became them.  Did
he ever ask himself if, in the face of all the
estrangements and difficulties of a marriage
that would naturally be objectionable to all
who loved him, the love now at fever-heat
would last ?   It may be questioned.

He lived in a dream.

Each day was like a bright bead upon a
string, beautiful as that which went before,
beautiful as that which was to come.  Time
lost for him its due proportions, only seeming
to exist when he was by Juanita's side, only
when he could watch the play of her beautiful face, listen to the halting music of her
tongue.

The " some Engleesh " that the girl had
boasted of on the occasion of their first meeting was gradually expanding and growing.

Love is a most stimulating teacher, and Juanita was an apt pupil.

"I love, thou lovest, we love." What can be easier than to learn these phrases off by heart?

Already had Cyril's love stood bravely a most trying test, for one evening, as he sat by Juanita's side, trying to guide her through the intricacies of an easy English book (Maritana, be it said once and for all, squatting on the doorstep of the vestibule, busy with a little tambour-frame like a miniature tambourine and laughing and muttering to herself as her manner was), the ugly head of Pedro Montalba was suddenly thrust through the little deeply-framed window in the offside of the room.

"Ah! it is mine oncle," said Juanita, and Cyril, flushing deeply red, sprang to his feet.

Making himself more round-shouldered than he was even by nature, with his elbows raised, his little fat hands outspread, his eyes mere slits with dark beads gleaming through, his face puckered into a thousand creases, the cigar-seller of the Piazza stood smiling and grimacing, while Lieutenant Peyton's fingers itched to take him by the throat and pitch him down head foremost among the prickly pears and aloe bushes.

"Do not dish-turb," he said, bowing many times in succession. "Do not of me make any account. You are wel-come, Sare Peyton, wel-come to my humble home. I am mooch glad to dank you for your gr-reat serveece to the señorita my niece. I did not before speak, becos these things are best kept what you call 'onder ze rose-tree.' It is not good to make plenty talk. Ah! no, ah! no, bettare not."

Then, leaving Cyril still struck speechless with the position in which he found himself, the old man appeared to fall foul suddenly of Maritana, and in a torrent of *patois*, half Spanish, half Italian, swept her and her tambour-frame forth as though with a besom. Then he strolled meditatively forth among the oranges and acacias, humming to himself as though he were an amiable humble-bee sipping the nectar of the flowers.

Cyril thought he could not be mistaken in recognising a pleading wistful pathos in Juanita's eyes as their great dark orbs were turned full upon him. He thought, too, that he could read that silent language, and he answered in a way generous and tender, if perhaps hardly prudent.

For the second time in his life he raised the fine olive-tinted fingers to his lips; nay, having once laid them so, he held them lingeringly, and saw that the girl thrilled and trembled at the contact.

He forgot all about old Pedro — was, perhaps, in the delirium of the moment, capable of thinking of that ancient schemer rather in the light of an acquisition than otherwise; forgot all the difficulties, draw-backs, complications, that beset him, and timorously—a great love is always timorous —drew the dark beauty to him, and kissed the sigh from her lips.

Almost before the girl could release herself

from his embrace, there was a soft flabby footfall on the pathway, and there stood Pedro, airily casting away the stump of a cheroot, airily contemplating the flight of a bird startled from the thicket of an orange-tree, airily smiling at and kissing his hand to Juanita, blind, or so it appeared, to her agitated condition of pale wonder and amaze.

She had been reared in a convent, under the gentle sway of nuns cunning in all women's handicraft, yet simple as the flowers that grew in their convent garden. She had heard no tales of love and war, of lady and of knight or troubadour, and now nature, speaking loudly in her heart, told her of a world of which she had never dreamed—a world of love and joy, a passionate delight in the nearness and presence of one supreme above all others, one whose voice was music, whose touch had magic in it. It was indeed the story of the Sleeping Princess.

Juanita's heart had slept. Now, at a touch, it had awakened.

From this day Cyril Peyton pursued his

course with his eyes open. No delusion was possible. He knew that Juanita was the niece of the cigar-seller; he even dimly re-cognised the fact that that worthy was play-ing a game—in other words, that his oily hands held certain cards, and that he was going to make the most of them.

Yet nothing weaned our young soldier from the love of Juanita. Away from her he was miserable, restless, ill at ease.

He might have said with Shakespeare's immortal lover—

> "I must hear from thee every day i' the hour,
> For in a minute there are many days."

All these things could not go entirely unnoticed in a community such as a garrison. Men are absolutely loyal to one another in such matters, and Gildea's mouth was sealed; but for all that, rumour grew, and it came to be a sort of understood thing that Peyton had "something on." In another this might not have been thought much of, but Peyton——

That was where the rub came in. Mrs.

Kershaw, grievously troubled by the hints brought to her by her husband from the mess-room, could not hide a certain anxious questioning that showed itself in her face and manner. Cyril, sincerely attached to her, and valuing her good opinion, felt this acutely, yet did not see his way to any explanation as yet.

He went to see her, just the same as ever, unheeding a touch of coldness visible in the greetings bestowed upon him by other ladies of the regiment whom he chanced to meet there. *She* was not cold to him; she was made of nobler stuff; so ran his thoughts.

"I will never give him up, Stanley, never!" said Mrs. Kershaw to her Major, and that doughty warrior replied—

"We will never give him up, Mary; he was so kind to little Alice."

One day Mrs. Kershaw sent Cyril a little note.

"Come and have tea with me this afternoon. I am sad to-day, and Major Kershaw is away on duty. You will know why I want you to come."

Then said Cyril to himself, "It is the day that little Alice died."

So he went.

She was very pale and quiet, that mother who never forgot that her little one was sleeping under the palm-trees; and the two met with the long close hand-clasp that means an intuitive sympathy of thought and feeling.

"Stanley said he was sure you would come if you could," she said, a tremble about her lips.

"I should think Major Kershaw might have known I should come, even if I couldn't," said Cyril earnestly.

Then they talked of little Alice, of her pretty ways and happy laughter in the days when she was well and strong; of her patient, quiet, strangely old-fashioned ways when the fever got hold of her, and she lay panting out her little life.

"Do you remember once, very, very near the end," said Mrs. Kershaw, pressing her hands one in the other to keep the tears from starting and overflowing, "how she stretched out her arms to you as you were going, and how she said, 'Kiss Alice once aden,' and you came back, and—O Cyril!—you kissed her dear little faded face—you kissed it many times?"

The tears would have their way now; the mother-heart could contain itself no longer.

Then, like a flash, it came over Cyril Peyton what all this meant. He was by his friend's side in a moment, and had taken her hand in his; he was looking straight, straight into the eyes that had watched him in his hour of sickness and pain. His voice shook; his hand, holding hers, was chill and cold.

"Believe me—believe me, dear Mrs. Kershaw, there never shall be anything in my life that shall make me unworthy of the love your dear one bore me; never anything that shall make me unworthy of the sacred kiss she gave me—the kiss that was her last good-bye."

Mrs. Kershaw was leaning her arm upon

the table, and had covered her drowned eyes with her hands. ·

"Do not heed what things you hear," went on Cyril, pleading. "Believe in me, trust me, you who have been my best friend; believe that even if I am——"

Here he halted, and she raised her head and looked at him through her tears.

"If you are in trouble, in perplexity, in doubt, can you not come and tell your troubles to my husband, he who is so wise and good, and would give you such good counsel? You are very dear to both of us —you know that, Cyril; you need not be afraid; and let me say one other—just one other word. When you were ill, do you remember begging me not to write and trouble Lady Peyton? Do you remember saying to me, 'You must not, because she could not bear it'? Think, then, are you going now to bring some trouble upon her that she cannot bear? I know not what is wrong with you. I ask no questions; I am not a curious woman; but I pray you think—think."

He would not let her go on.

He caught her hand and raised it to his lips.

"You are so good to me," he said, and she was sure there was a sob in his voice, "so good—you and he. I know you would do anything, either of you ; but no one can help me now—no one. The time may come when you can, but I do not know. There, let me go. I hear the sound of wheels; some one is coming. I am not fit to meet any one. God bless you for your kindly words, dear, dear friend. God bless you, now and always!"

Mrs. Kershaw had a wonderful faculty for picking herself up, and managed to meet her new visitors with well-assumed composure, but the haggard beauty of Cyril's face, the pathos of his voice, haunted her as the echo of sad music lingers with us when the strain is silent.

"You have done all you can. That sort of thing cannot be said twice over," was the Major's verdict on this interview.

About a month later, when the days were

growing hot and long, and men who could get leave grasped at it promptly and eagerly, a new element was added to Cyril's visits to the grey-walled villa.

He noticed a long-coated darkly-clad figure loitering round the sunny garden—a figure that might well have stepped out of some old-world story, where the *curé* of the village is the central figure of the place—the guide, philosopher, and friend of every man, woman, and child in it.

An aquiline clear-cut face, close shaven, with a mobile mouth, and thin grey hair falling on either side; a tall slender hollow-chested figure, and, in strange contradistinction to all the rest, eyes keen as steel and dark as sloes, astute, penetrating, yet kindly.

This was the face that, from under a wide slouched hat of sombre black, looked at Cyril, as the priest at last brought his wanderings to an end, and came up under the shady verandah that topped the vestibule entrance.

"Padre Sebastiano," said Juanita in an

awed voice, and the priest uncovered, looked keenly yet furtively into the young Englishman's face, and then held out his long nervous hand—a concession to British manners and customs.

Cyril felt ill at ease. There is something strangely antipathetic to the robust English mind in these foreign priests, in their restrained ways and epicene appearance. Prejudice is ready to spring to arms; distrust lurks round the corner; so we may as well say at once that no more simple saintly soul existed than that of Padre Sebastiano, that he was absolutely innocent and ignorant of any plot or plots on the part of Pedro Montalba, cigar-seller and usurer, and was but bent upon defending the gentle lamb of his flock from the ravening wolf—in other words, from the young Englishman, whose face recalled to his mind a picture of the beloved disciple over a side-altar in the Church of our Lady of Pity.

Bows and friendly gestures were at length exchanged, and then the good father betook himself to the garden and his Book of Hours.

"He baptized me into Holy Church," said Juanita, whose studies in the English language had now made immense progress. "He is so good, so good; and when I was so small as so," indicating a liliputian height indeed, " I take his fingare in my leetle hand, and learn to walk one, two, tree leetle steps; then he clap the hands so, and laugh, and Maritana cry, she so much glad."

Cyril became so used to the sight of Padre Sebastiano that he took no more heed of him than he did of Maritana or her ancient spouse, and oh! the happy days that came and went, the loving greetings and the tender partings, the longings when away, the sweet content when near! Juanita sang to the mandoline, and what a picture she made, with her dainty feet on a little stool (all tambour-work done by Maritana's own hands), her mandoline upon her knee, and her scarlet lips parted to let the sweet low song run on! Was it any wonder that her lover watched her with adoring eyes?

What wonder that he forgot all difference of creed and station, all obstacles present and to come ?

Meanwhile Pedro watched and waited.

He was a bad old man, as we know, but the bad are not all bad. There is often a sweet ripe spot to be found in the rottenest pear; and in Pedro's black heart, amid all its lust for gain, was one jewel set: he loved his niece Juanita.

She was the child of his only sister, who had married far above her own station in life— been a most unhappy wife and died young, confiding her infant to his care. He had been faithful, had this bad old Pedro, faithful and true to the behest of the dead. The child had been reared by Maritana, once the mother's nurse; then, when old enough, sent to a convent of the highest class, where she had been taught all needful accomplishments to grace a gentlewoman.

What more could Pedro do ?

Yet more he did.

He kept the girl pure and free from all

the contamination that might have assailed
her in the floating society of a garrison town.
He never used her—as men of his class will
sometimes use the women belonging to them
—as a decoy, an attractive light to bring
moths about the candle. She could not have
been better guarded had she been the daughter of a king.

Of late Pedro had been restless and strange
in his manner, starting at a sudden footstep,
drawing his breath deep if an acquaintance
tapped him on the shoulder from behind.

Pedro was cruising in deep and stormy
waters.

He had been gambling in a big way; he
had lost; ruin had stared him in the face—
ruin for himself, ruin for Juanita. He had
staved off the evil day by a nefarious—nay,
a criminal transaction. He fancied himself
safe; he was not, however, sure. Some safe
retreat, some trustworthy guardian, must be
found for "Bambinetta" (his love-name for
Juanita).

He heard the story of young Peyton's

adventure, his visit to the walled-in house. He read the story told by the girl's changing face : love—love at first sight.

"It is good," he said to himself. "He is a heretic, *basta!* but he is honest. He will marry her ; he will love her always. The English love their wives like that ; they are droll ; but it is good."

So while all the world—the little world of the garrison—wondered, while Mary Kershaw thought of little Alice, and prayed that all harm might be kept from the man who had been her loving friend, Cyril lived his idyll, and the days were golden with sunshine, and the nights pure silver with moonlight ; the music of the mandoline throbbed in the slumberous air, and the white blossom on the orange-trees turned to amber fruit in Juanita's garden.

Then, just when Pedro began to think himself really safe, the crash came. The news ran like wildfire through the town.

The cigar divan was barred and darkened, the gay striped awnings that were wont to span the verandah were furled, and Pedro Montalba had been taken away in the night by the secret police.

When Cyril reached the villa—poor Caliph in a lather that later on made Dorrington's hair ready to stand on end—Maritana was waiting for him, her head thrown back, her body swaying to and fro, a horrible grinding, moaning sound coming from her lips—a keening such as no Irishwoman, however practised, could attain to.

Suddenly she looked up, sprang up, shrieked out loud, and fled into the garden, leaving Cyril to follow.

What silence! what desolation! And there upon the floor of the vestibule, like a robe thrown carelessly and aimlessly down, lies something eerie and terrible.

A dark head is prone; two white hands, clasped, are outstretched above it.

"Juanita! Juanita! my sweet, my darling!" cries Cyril, and the girl rises, staggers to her feet, and flings herself into his eager outstretched arms.

"Ceereel! Ceereel! I have no one now but you—no one now but you!"

Then the inner door that is at the top of a shallow flight of steps opens, and the priest, very pale and calm, comes quietly in.

# CHAPTER III.

## BLOTTED OUT.

UNDER the breath of summer Scarsdale-in-the-Dale grew with each day more and more beautiful. There is a point in the year's perfection, as there is in every human life, at which progress seems to stand still—to bask, as it were, in the high noon of perfection attained to.

The corn, green and full, stood thickly on the slopes; the dells were carpeted with flowers and nodding grasses, and by the mill the hedges were wreathed with honeysuckle, while the purple clusters of the blackberries nodded at you as you passed; the meadowsweet rose tall and slender from the very brink of the rushing mill-stream, and the blue veronica crept down to the water's edge as if to kiss the ripples as they stole gently in among the grass.

How contentedly the miller's ducks dabbled with their bills in the shallows, or waddled up the narrow pathway, one after another in single file, uttering that low, pensive "quack" that is surely the very happiest and most complacent of sounds!

It was Christmas-time, snow-time, when last we saw Scarsdale; but there had not been much to talk about in the interval (save the probable yield of crops), and the oak-tree parliament had languished somewhat. The new curate had long since become the old curate, and no one wondered any more at the natural history excursions taken by himself and his dapper little wife, or the fact of their being seen fishing with nets in certain stagnant pools, tributaries of the river, where lurked water-newts, dyticus beetles, and other kindred creatures, or being met carrying little cans in which the quarry were imprisoned.

The usual number of children had fallen off the high side-walks in Upper Scarsdale, with the results of broken noses and pates;

the usual number of topers had been brought before the constable ; Mother Bond had continued her erratic course of life, and was still watching for Danny, who never came.

There was nothing to discuss in all these common-place occurrences, and as to a mortal quarrel between Maister Straw and Pilkington, that had been threshed out long ago. A faint rumour as to the expectation of an heir to the house of Peyton made some slight variety, but the announcement in the one London paper taken in at the Golden Crown of "The wife of Launcelot Peyton, Esq., of a son, still-born," set that at rest.

"Happen it be's t' curse as Mother Bond set on Sir Marmadook," said a bent and quavering old man—a sort of human tripod, since he could not stir an inch without his stick.

There was an uneasy silence at this, and even that buxom widow, the landlady, laid a finger on her lip ; but the tripod was unconscious of antagonism in the air. He pottered over the paper, gazing at it through a venerable pair of spectacles framed in horn, and following each line with a trembling finger.

"Still-born," he said — "still-born. You means as it didna' cry. Moine wur not made that way. No, no; they let me an' my missis know as they wur theer, alive an' kickin', that did they," and he chuckled to himself, shaking perilously with the effort. "Bo' it's like enoo as it be's t' curse as Mother Bond set on Sir Marmydook."

"Howd thee noise!" roared a stalwart farmer from a far corner. "It's ill luck to be talkin' o' witches' curses and suchlike fearsome things, and 'as been known to breed 'em."

The landlady nodded, well pleased at this. She had three little ones asleep upstairs, and you never knew. Of course it might be all old women's tales, and yet—— Better err on the safe side, and let Mother Bond be.

Just then there came a low tapping at the "cosy" window.

The evening had closed in grey and moon-

less, and the red curtain had been drawn
and the lamp lit. Its light shone with a
ruddy pleasant glow, and made a pretty bit
in the still grey landscape.

At the sound of the tapping fingers the
man nearest the window pulled the curtain
aside, and the eerie face of Mother Bond
was seen pressed against the glass, peering
in. The men all huddled into one corner,
the poor tripod losing his stick and his
balance in one fell moment, and sinking a
helpless heap all among the legs of the rest.

As to the landlady, she threw her frilled
apron over her head, and ran upstairs to the
room where lay her sleeping cherubs, locked
and barred the door, and took the still further
precaution of setting her back against it.

Meanwhile down below the sturdy farmer
at last summoned up courage, extricated
himself from his brother topers, and stealing out into the passage, cautiously opened
the door.

"Have any on yo' seen my boy Danny?"
came Mother Bond's voice, shrill and wild,

and then with a shriek of eldritch laughter the old woman flitted to the seat round the parliament oak, and crouched there, hugging herself.

The men came out one by one and formed a timorous group, seen in the fitful glimmer of the swaying light that depended from the Golden Crown itself.

The poor tripod had well-nigh been left behind, but he shrieked out for some one to "set him on his legs," and for some one else to find his stick; and, these things being done, shambling and staggering, he joined the rest.

"Oo'll flout us an' fleer us, an' happen cast a spell on us," he quavered, curious yet dismayed.

"Howd thee noise!" roared the rest, a request so often made to the poor tripod that it might be wondered he ever spoke at all.

"We's tak' thy stick awa' if thou says owt else," said the farmer in so laboriously low a voice that he grew crimson with the effort; "an' thee knows it's all very well to ask for to be set upon thy legs, but they're a poor sort to trust to, and as wayward as Andy's here when he's trying to get whoam Saturdays, and 'is legs is of another moind from hissel'!"

"Never a son, never a son," chanted the old woman, swaying herself backward and forward, and looking as though there was blood upon her hair and face from the red light of the curtained window that fell upon her.

"I tellt yo' it wur her as made t' babe born still, so it couldna cry."

To bundle the tripod into a chair and take his stick from him, in spite of his squeaking like a rat—in fact, to convert him into a helpless wriggling biped, was the work of a moment, and then the rest listened awestruck to Mother Bond's mutterings.

As at last she rose, they fell back a bit; but she passed them by, her arms lifted high, waving and beckoning, above her head. The hood of her cloak had fallen back, and her white and withered face looked up to the dim grey heavens.

She was still beckoning, beckoning, as she went along, still chanting some wild inarticulate song, to the rhythm of which she stepped. They stole on after her, the bravest first, the most timid last.

The landlady, with her back against the door upstairs, and the biped helpless in the corner, were the only denizens of the Golden Crown. Fear is a mighty passion, but I think curiosity—a good healthy curiosity—is a mightier still.

One of the men, drifting from his companions, came up alongside the scudding grey figure.

"What are yo' calling fur, Mother Bond?" said he. "Be it t' mune as yo're a-beckonin' for?"

She turned on him so fiercely that he cowered as if he had been struck.

"Ill news—news to drag their hearts out—that's what I'm callin'. Ill news from over the sea—ill news! See, see!" as a bat circled wildly round her head; "there it comes, there it comes—ill news from over the sea!" Then, with a sudden change of tone, "Have any on yo' seen my boy Danny?"

"Well, I'm danged!" said the farmer, slapping his thigh till the solid flesh rang again. "Hoo be's same as a cluckin' 'en—same as a cluckin' 'en. Cluck! cluck! cluck! after that theer good-for-nowt."

"Hush up!" cried the rest; "there's times she's wiser than she looks, and happen she'll cast a spell."

Even as he spoke she turned upon them, stretching forth her fingers fork-wise, and in a trice they were round the other side the great oak, all shoving for the middlemost place. It comforted their hearts like wine when they heard the weird, uncanny chaunt of the witch, making night hideous once more: "Ill news—ill news, come across the sea!" for they knew Mother Bond was off and away, waving her lean arms, and calling on the familiar spirits that were popularly

believed to bear her company on all occasions, though invisible to the eyes of ordinary
mortals.

It was a strange sight to see first one and
then another grizzled face peering cautiously
forth, touched with a ruddy glow, as the
shimmer from the red curtain fell across
it.   Now on this side of the oak-tree, now
on that, the peepers peeped, and at length,
all being silent, figure after figure stole slowly
and softly forth, treading as if on eggs, and
so made for the Golden Crown.   The tripod
having by aid of the poker regained his
stick, came forth wavering, just in time to
be shoved back by the in-comers, and told
—quite as if the idea were something new,
and had just struck everybody—to "How'd
his noise."

The landlady had now ventured as far as
the stair-head, and soon joined her guests
below, where a babel of tongues and discussion, description, and narration prevailed until
"closing time" came round, when, with many
a glance up the road this way, and down the

road that way, the worthies betook themselves home.

Then the ruddy glow died out with a jerk; the glimmer of the landlady's candle was seen flickering up the stairs, and the Golden Crown was at rest for the night.

The moon, on the contrary, was just about getting up; not much of a moon, perhaps, still a pretty silver crescent, something like a lady's brooch, making a pale, diffused patch of light in the drifting veil of grey clouds. At this a tiny blackcap, hoping, maybe, that he might be taken for a nightingale by people who knew no better, set up his pretty gurgling song.

Besides touching the windows of the Golden Crown, the faint radiancy of the young moon shone bright on the mullioned panes of the Old Hall, where, through one that was set back upon its hasp, came stealing out into the quiet night the sound of a woman's voice singing.

We have seen this picture before, in the " mind's eye " of Cyril Peyton—the piano not

far from the window, the pale pure face upraised, the lace-encircled hands pressing the
ivory keys.

Sir Marmaduke was away at some political
dinner, and my Lady had all the old house to
herself.

That "light at eventide," of which she had
spoken to the Rector on that rosy Christmas
Eve, which none of us will have forgotten,
had for her gone on with its still shining
through the waking days of spring and the
golden days of summer. The sense that her
boy was nearer to her, that within an appreci-
able time she should once more see his bonnie
face, hear his cheery, loving voice, wrapped
her round like a robe of light. Hard words,
cruel insinuations, coldness, the bitter tenets
of a creed made not by God, but for God—
what were these things to her? They were
but as empty sounds in her ears, and seemed
to have lost their power to wound.

"Marion," said Sir Marmaduke one day,
"I do believe that the wholesome discipline
of having the desire of your eyes taken from

you, the idol you had set between your soul and heaven rent from your hold, has taught you at last the lesson of submission."

She only smiled, and bent her head as though in acknowledgment of some courtier-like compliment. Why should she tell her husband that hope, not submission, was taming her wild unrest; that a steadfast looking forward to the termination of her trial, not a resignation to its bitterness, was the staff on which she leaned? It had not pleased Sir Marmaduke that his son Cyril should be despatched from India to Gibraltar, but he had sense enough to realise that in the service these chances are inevitable, and quite beyond the control of private individuals. Besides, Lance was married, mortgages were being paid off; other claims were dwindling as large payments were made; the financial atmosphere was clearing rapidly. Above all, that little heap of yellow ashes had been scattered to the winds of heaven long since.

Any folly that might ever have held possession of Launcelot's mind as to Alison

Darling would have been fostered by the silly sentimentality to which Cyril was prone —had, indeed, been so fostered ; but now all danger of that kind was past. True, there was a gloom about Lance at times that Sir Marmaduke would rather not have seen, and made him regret that so much of his own past life lay in his son's hand—a black piece of knowledge enough. And this son, still-born, a mere blank and nonentity in the roll-call of life—that, too, was a vexation ; but Lance and his wife were young people, and doubtless a long line of Peytons would yet flourish at Ellerslie. Sometimes Sir Marmaduke had a suspicion that the Lady Jane was not so strong and healthful as a young woman ought to be. Of course you could not expect her to be like the Rector's daughter, for instance, whose springing elastic tread would carry her miles unwearied, and whose cheek showed the tint of the heart of a rose—well, perhaps not of late, not just of late. There had been a change in the girl, no one could deny that,

since—well, since Lance married. Perhaps,
after all, there was more love and less
ambition in that foolish business which
had happily died a natural death than he—
Sir Marmaduke—had supposed. That letter
had been a lucky hit; it had got the Rector's
back up, and made things sure. Still, the
blood of the Peytons revolted against the
means used; and Sir Marmaduke, in re
volving the matter over in his own mind,
marvelled if "that little whelp Westerton"
could have penned the offensive missive, or,
if that ornament to the Church were not
the guilty party, then who might be? He
fully admitted the heinous nature of the
action, though justifying himself in the using
of a vile tool that had suited his purpose
only too well.

Both the existence of the letter and the use
that had been made of it were facts hidden
from Lady Peyton's knowledge. It would
never have crossed the Rector's mind to give
even a hint to her on either matter, and Sir
Marmaduke kept silence from an inherent

feeling of shame; though no earthly power
could have induced him to plead guilty to
such a weakness. Unconscious, then, of the
storms that played around her, Lady Peyton
had gone serenely on her way, cheered and
heartened by that new light of hope to which
allusion has already been made. Cyril's
letters too; there had been a change in them.
It was as though they were bathed in light!
A deeper tone, like the vibrating thrill of a
deep-voiced instrument, was perceptible running through them. She had written to him
of her almost childish joy in his comparative
nearness to her now; he had written back,
answering as some sweet echo might have
done to a song-bird's cry.

There were other influences also that had
come into her life at this time to brighten
it. Lady Jane had proved to be a loving
and thoughtful character, and was much
drawn towards the mother of her husband,
and Lance (still possessed with that idea of
something owing to his mother for the faulty
years of the past) was pleased that this

should be so, and it came about that Lady
Peyton talked of Cyril to his brother's wife,
and, in some sort, showed something of
her own heart to those gentle eyes. Being
also a woman of keen intuition, Lady Jane
gathered ideas of her mother-in-law's life,
and—not without repulsion—grasped a con-
ception of Sir Marmaduke's character, and
of the fanaticism that had fallen on him
like a blight. Not that she gathered much
of this from any words that fell from her
husband's lips, for Lance kept a strange
silence about his father; starting away, as
it were, from the subject as one might from
the touch of a hand upon a still tender
wound. Lady Jane, too, had her own trials.
Lance was a kind, affectionate husband,
patient with her in her delicate health to
an extent rare in a man ; but yet——

The sound of his step, the echo of his voice,
were as music in the ears of Lady Jane ;
without him by her side there was a silence
that nothing could fill. When his moody
fits were on him—and this was not seldom.

—the sun was darkened for her, and she knew no rest. Worst of all was the fact that she was helpless to minister to him. All he craved for at such times was solitude and silence.

She had hoped that baby fingers would woo him to a closer life with her; but now the memory of the little waxen effigy of what should have been a living, breathing child, the tiny form so still and cold, with closed eyes and little dead hands piteously helpless-looking, that they had let her see for a moment ere it was taken from her sight for ever, was all that remained to her.

Lady Peyton had grieved over this little life's failure. She was not without the knowledge that Lance had drifted more and more since his marriage; that those gloomy spells were upon him oftener; and she, too, had hoped much from the presence of a little child in the home that was often far too silent.

Yet even here her thoughts of Cyril came to her, thrilled through and through with hope.

When Cyril should come, then Lance would cheer up and look at life with less weary eyes.

When Cyril should come, then the sun would shine, and the birds would sing, and the bells in the old church tower would ring with a sweeter chime.

And so it came to pass that on this grey-veiled night, with its crescent moon, the mother's thoughts flew across the great and wide sea to the land where the great Rock is washed by the purple waves. All the more did they fly to her darling, because all at once Cyril's letters had stopped.

We know what it is to wait and watch for those messengers from over seas, the letters of our dear ones who are far away. We know the sickening disappointment of watching and waiting in vain.

First one mail day had passed, then another, and still no letter came.

But to-morrow—to-morrow would bring happier luck; to-morrow would make fears seem things of folly, things to be laughed at, derided, mocked at.

How quiet the house was!

Hound lying at his lady's feet, whimpered as though the heavy silence irked him.

My Lady laid her hand upon his head and told him that a letter would come to-morrow.

Then once more she touched the keys of the piano, and memories of Cyril's boyhood crowded round her like flocking spirits.

"Do you remember—do you remember," said each one, urgent to tell its own little story first. And so she was led on to the melody of the song her boy had loved—

" Su passaggieri, venite via !
Santa Lucia—Santa Lucia ! "

How well the soft swing of the refrain suited the still grey night! How sweet was the voice of the singer! How full the heart from which the music rose!

The silver crescent was seen no more; night reigned, and hall and cottage alike slept, with curtains, like closed eyelids, veiling every window; but soon the faint greenish light of the new day began to tinge the east, and the birds were astir, rustling among the branches with agitated mutterings, as though a new day had never been born before and the matter required serious consultation.

In Scarsdale village about the first house to lift its sleepy lids was the post-office, and the first excitement of the day was the arrival of her Majesty's mails, as represented by a remarkably rough, unkempt Shetland pony, and an equally unkempt boy, with a sack secured with heavy seals thrown across his saddle-bow. To this cargo he held on like grim death, plainly under the impression that instant execution would be his fate should any mischance happen to it—indeed, the constable had many times given him ghastly warnings in that direction, and Maister Straw had solemnly assured him that "men had been hanged for less."

No wonder, then, the post-boy was serious and wide-eyed, and given to heaving a great sigh of relief as he banged the sack on the sorting-table and touched his forelock to the postmistress.

"I'm glad," said that worthy woman to her spouse on this particular morning of which we are now telling—"I'm glad there's letters for the Old Hall from that there outlandish place where Mr. Cyril is. Mrs. Dutton told me as how her Ladyship was sorely put out about none comin' this two weeks or more. Here's one for Sir Marmadook and one for my Lady. That's as it should be."

Lady Peyton was one of those women who manage, almost unconsciously, to win the devotion of their dependents, and who are served not for greed, but for love, and it may be safely said that the under-gardener from the Hall, whose duty it was to fetch the letter-bag, put—as the saying goes—his best leg foremost when the postmistress told him that letters from Mr. Cyril were contained therein.

"As usual, the letter-bag was taken to Sir Marmaduke's study, after which all subsequent proceedings were wholly unprecedented and out of rule.

My Lady, waiting in the library for her husband to come in to breakfast—curbing her impatience as to the contents of the letter-bag as best she might, betraying herself only, indeed, by a slight increase of pallor and quickening of breath—was startled by a ringing peal upon Sir Marmaduke's bell.

As she sprang to her feet, Mrs. Dutton, pale and frightened, hurried into the room.

"My Lady," she said, "my Lady, Sir Marmaduke wants you to go to him in the study. Let me go too—oh, my dear Lady, let me go too!"

Lady Peyton did not seem to hear. She walked steadily and slowly to the door, and poor Mrs. Dutton, taking the law into her own hands, followed.

"It is something about Master Cyril," she said to the butler, also scared and agitated. "I am sure it is. Oh, it will kill my Lady; I know it will!"

Somehow—Mrs. Dutton always said she really didn't know exactly how—she followed her mistress as far as the study door, saw Sir Marmaduke with an open letter in his hand, and a look of wild white rage upon his face, and then found herself shut out, all shaking with fear, in the corridor.

For Lady Peyton there was no such shelter.

She stood before her husband, pale indeed, yet showing no sign of fear.

It was not the first time she had seen him carried away by a tempest of undisciplined rage.

Cyril had made him angry, how she knew not; the letter in his hand was in Cyril's writing. She must be patient, and allay the storm if she could.

For a time Sir Marmaduke appeared to be choked by his own passion, so that clear utterance was impossible to him.

But at last he spoke.

"Marion—your son—our son—has disgraced himself—disgraced himself beyond all hope of redemption."

"Disgraced!" she cried. "No, Marmaduke, not that—not disgraced."

" Wilful woman," he answered, beside himself at contradiction, "do not dare to gain-
say me. I tell you he is disgraced, and from
this day I swear he shall be no son of mine
—no son of yours."

"He is my son—he will be my son—
always—no matter what he has done."

Slender, fragile, yet invincible, she stood
before him, her noble head raised, her hands
clasped before her.

"What has he done?" she said. "Tell me
that—it is my due."

"He has married the niece of a blackguard
and a usurer; he has married a Papist, and
given to her our honourable name."

"Folly—hot-headed folly, I doubt not,
Marmaduke—but not disgrace. If he had
ruined the girl, that would have been disgrace,
but—not this."

He looked as though he could have felled
her where she stood, turned from her as from
some sight that sickened him, put his hand
upon the bell, and then a second peal rang
through the house.

It was answered by the butler.

"Tell Mrs. Dutton to fetch the big Bible from the stand in her Ladyship's room, and do you return here also."

"Marmaduke, what is it you would do?" said Lady Peyton, a great terror now filling her eyes; "do nothing rashly. Oh, my husband! take no rash vow upon your head. Cyril is young—the young are easily led. Have some mercy, even as you hope yourself for mercy!"

"Silence!" he thundered. "I know not if this sorrow and shame have not been brought upon you in judgment for your idol-worship—your undisciplined——"

But she would not bate one inch of her ground; she would not have the words stifled on her lips.

"There is sorrow," she said, "but not shame."

"Is it not shame that your son should marry a Papist—a low designing creature?"

"We know nothing. Do not judge her——"

He felt this passive resistance to be maddening. Heaven knows what furious words he might have hurled at his wife's devoted head ; but at that moment the door opened, and the butler—very white and scared—entered the room bearing the big family Bible, while Mrs. Dutton followed, wringing her apron into a perfect whip in the agony of the moment.

.Sir Marmaduke turned the pages of the heavy volume with slow deliberation until he came to the place where the births of his two sons were recorded. Lady Peyton stood by the great desk, her hand resting there, her eyes following her husband's every movement.

With perfect deliberation he selected a pen, dipped it carefully in the ink, and drew a thick black line through the name of his younger son Cyril.

"Witness," he said to the two scared servitors, who by this time had huddled together as if for protection, though Mrs. Dutton's eyes never left her mistress's face—"witness,

both of you, that from this day Lady Peyton
and myself have no son—save one."

Mrs. Dutton broke out into bitter weeping,
but Lady Peyton was calm.

She had caught sight of a second letter,
addressed to herself in the dear well-known
handwriting. There Cyril had told all his
tale; there his mother would read between
the lines, and learn how to make excuses for
his error.

The name of his son thus blotted out, Sir
Marmaduke turned to his wife—

"You have sworn to obey me; you have
told me many times that you strive to live up
to that vow taken before your God. Madam,
remember from this day that Cyril Peyton is
no son of yours. I forbid you to write to
him, or to acknowledge him in any way. Let
him and his Papist wife drift whither they
will. They are nothing to you or to me."

At last, poor mother, she was broken down.

She came close to his side, and looked up
into his face with agonised eyes.

"Do not put it like that," she pleaded.

"It is to manacle me, to bind me down, and you know it. Oh, husband, have mercy!"

"You waste your words," he said, carelessly turning from her. "What I have said, I have said, and now, to show you that my words are not mere empty things——"

A small fire of pine-knots burnt in the wide open grate, and in another moment Cyril's unopened letter to his mother was curling and twisting like a living tortured thing among the spurting flames.

With a cry Lady Peyton darted forward, but Sir Marmaduke caught her by the wrists, and held her firmly back, the while Dutton's sobs resounded through the room; and Hound, throwing back his mighty head, gave tongue as though he, too, were keening for the beloved one whose name had just been blotted out.

# CHAPTER IV.

## THE RUBY HEART.

It has been said that Scarsdale was a sleepy place. It was not, however, allowed any prolonged slumber just now.

The lamentable marriage made by Sir Marmaduke Peyton's younger son, the fact that his father had "disowned" him, together with other remarkable features of the case, some true and some untrue, agitated the village as a high wind sways and stirs a forest.

It may be imagined what an oak-tree parliament was held on the matter itself, and upon the still more interesting fact that Mother Bond had known the ill news was on the way, and beckoned it, and called to it "same as if it wur a burred." A Papist was a fearsome thing, and no one would wonder if they heard that poor Master Cyril was tied to a stake and burned up; but a cunning witch right in their midst was more fearsome still. It behoved them all to be on the best of terms with Mother Bond, and ready to do any little handy job that might suggest itself at that tumble-down old place she lived in.

As for the lady of the Old Hall, who was ever ready with help and comfort in the day of their own sorrow and sickness; what could they do for her?

They could make bold to stand close alongside the walk through the churchyard, and pull their caps off as she passed; she was mighty quick to see things, and would understand "quick enoo," that would she. Sir Marmaduke was a hard man (this was said in hushed voices and with heads very close together), and "a mother's a mother," said one. This being looked upon as rather a profound remark, another put in his oar, and said, with grave shakings of the head, "Aye, an' a choilt's a choilt," which was also received as a pithy saying, significant of much.

Thus lured on, the tripod made a venture.

"A Pappist's a terribul thing, safe and sure, mates; but happen she wur a purty Pappist, wha' knows?"

"Howd thee noise!" they cried in concert; "if t' parson heerd thee, wheer wouldst ta be?"

Which was doing a cruel injustice to Mr. Darling, the widest-minded and most charitable of men.

How can we tell of the sorrow at the Rectory over Cyril's trouble? They called it "trouble," not disgrace, as some did. In their eyes Cyril could not disgrace himself.

"Oh, papa," said Alison, "to think of him, so bright and good, so sweet and gentle to dear mamma, and now disowned, cast off; and poor Lady Peyton—— I scarcely dared to lift my eyes to her when she passed us on Sunday, every one feeling for her so deeply, and no one daring to say a word. Papa, did you see those men standing by the pathway bareheaded as she went by? Wasn't it beautiful, papa? And she so quiet, the very sweep of her dress full of dignity, and her face, and then the lesson for the day—the story of Benjamin. I never felt afraid for you before—afraid, I mean, that you would break down—but your voice seemed to sink and fail."

"As my heart, failed and fainted within me for very pity," said the Rector. "The knowledge of the silent suffering that was so near me almost unmanned me."

"But, papa," said Alison, "things cannot go on like this always; time does such wonders, softens things so much."

"My dear, my dear," said the Rector, patting the hand that lay near him upon the table, "my own little girl!"

He knew that time had softened Alison's trouble; but he knew also that the light-hearted girl of yore existed no more; he knew that a radiance had died out from his darling's eyes, a buoyancy from her spirit, to return no more, for the woman who once has loved and lost and suffered can never again be the same. The music of her life may have gained deeper and sweeter notes, but its merry ring is gone.

"Well, you know that it is so. God is good, papa, and will not let us suffer above that we are able, and I am sure Sir Marmaduke's anger will die down. It will—it must, and dear Cyril will come back to the home of his boyhood. Ah! yes, papa, and bring his pretty wife (I am sure she is pretty) with him. I will not say that he will come back to his mother's heart, for he has never been banished from that; but we shall see the light of joy dawn once more in her dear, sad eyes, that are so much more beautiful than any girl's; we shall see her as we used to see her in the olden days coming through the churchyard with Cyril by her side."

The girl's voice faltered as she prophesied these joyous things, and the Rector, making her no answer, walked to the window, and stood gazing out at the glory of "mamma's garden," now all ablaze with flowers of every hue.

But it may be questioned if he saw them very clearly.

He could not raise himself to the hopeful view of things taken by Alison. He understood better than she did the bitterness of fanaticism, the vengeful hatred, the vehement antagonism of which Sir Marmaduke was capable.

Sir Marmaduke might, in time, be brought to pardon the social status, or rather want of status, of his son's wife—her creed, never.

Mr. Darling knew more still.

He knew how the jealousy of a lifetime was now finding full vent and scope; he knew that Cyril, the bright-eyed, sunny-hearted boy, had vexed his father all his days. The gloomy tenets of Calvinism had slidden from the boy's nature as water from the bright plumage of a tropical bird ; they found no possible echo in a nature as far removed from any taint of morbidity or pessimism as it was possible to be. Antagonism reigned between these two, father and son, from the first, and the devotion of the mother

to the Benjamin of the family had also done
its work.

A student of human nature, Mr. Darling
recognised the fact that the more indigna-
tion and hostility became legitimate, the
more Sir Marmaduke revelled in the outlet
for the spleen of years. He said to his own
soul that he " did well to be angry ; " his sense
of righteousness was satisfied, and ran com-
placently alongside his seething wrath.

But the Rector could not find in his heart
to denounce his girl's fond fancies as mere
castles in the air, void of all foundation in
truth. He drummed softly on the pane,
and Alison, chilled by his silence, spoke no
more, resting her head on her hand, and
setting herself to wondering how Lance would
take this news, assuring herself that he would
bravely and nobly come forward as a mediator,
and, unheeding of hard words or cold looks,
plead with Sir Marmaduke for the absent.
Even when a woman's love for a man must
needs be bankrupt indeed, her faith in him
will remain, and be to her an impersonal

and chastened joy. Ever sensitive to an abnormal extent, poor Mrs. Darling had been completely broken down by this sudden news of Cyril, and it may even be questioned whether the fact of his wife being a " Papist " did not come home to her with as deep a repulsion as to Sir Marmaduke himself. She had not thought out life's many problems as deeply as her husband, nor had she attained to that widespread catholicity and charity of mind that sees good in all things. On being told gently and tenderly of what had happened, she at once took to her bed, read and re-read those letters of Cyril's that had been at all times such welcome messengers, and finally delivered herself of an opinion that the girl was " a designing creature," and poor dear Cyril a victim to be passionately pitied.

Finding that reasoning with her was useless, the Rector and Alison very wisely gave up the attempt, and this was how it came about that " mamma's room " was empty, save for the father and daughter, and mamma's sofa displayed nothing more

than a prettily embroidered coverlet neatly
folded.

The silence that fell upon Alison's last words
was strangely enough broken, the Rector's
musings appositely enough interrupted, for a
servant entering announced—

"Lady Peyton, if you please, sir, is in your
study. She asked for you particular, and I
showed her in there."

"Oh, papa, papa," said Alison, clasping her
hands, "it is something about Cyril!"

The Rector made a gesture enjoining silence,
and left the room.

As he entered his study, Lady Peyton rose
to meet him.

Her heavy veil of black crape was thrown
back, showing up the noble mask of her
marble-white face in high relief. Her eyes
had a strange far-off look even when they
met yours, as though they watched across
the sea for what would never come. The
Rector took her hand and kept it, its chill
touch thrilling him through.

He was so agitated by her whole appearance that he scarce could find any words to speak to her. She saw his trouble, and a pale flitting smile just stirred her lips—a smile that seemed to thank him for his sympathy, yet in some way conveyed to him how far that sympathy, or any other, was from reaching the core of her sorrow.

"You have come to me——" said Mr. Darling at last, gathering himself together with an effort.

"I have come to you for help," she put in quickly; "I know that none ever come to you in vain for that."

Again that little flickering smile that affected him so deeply; the cold hand pressed his, and was withdrawn.

"If I can do anything to be of comfort to you, dear Lady Peyton, you know——"

"Yes, I know," she said, again interrupting him; "I know quite well. If I had not known I should not have come. See," she went on, drawing a little square case from the pocket of her cloak, "I want you to send this to my son Cyril."

"To send it for you?" said the Rector.

She opened the case, and there glittering with the crimson glow of blood, lay a ruby heart—a heart cut out of a single stone —a jewel flawless, rich, and beautiful.

"No; to send it as it is, without a word; he—Cyril—will know all that it means."

She swayed slightly as she spoke, and the Rector put out his hand to support her; but she recovered herself marvellously, and set the little case upon the table, where, a ray of sunshine catching the gem within, it shone like a globe of crimson fire.

"I want it sent quickly," she said, and he could see her lips tremble, "quickly— to-night, if possible. The mail leaves London to-morrow."

"Am I to send no message?"

"None, Mr. Darling. I am forbidden to hold any communication with my son—forbidden to put pen to paper to him. I dare not fly in the face of this command, I must not; it would be to falsify my whole life. But I want this glowing heart to carry its silent message to my boy — my boy, dear friend, my own, own boy, mind, whatever he may have done.

"May I say that much?"

"There is no need; he will know, and words are forbidden to me. I must overcome myself, I must submit; night and day I pray for strength and grace. You will pray for me, too, will you not? I stand in sore need—sore, sore need. Sometimes I am tempted to say : 'My sorrow is greater than I can bear.'"

He turned away, unable to look at her rapt pale face.

"Nay," she said, pitifully pleading, "you must not fail me. I look to you to help and strengthen me. I try to hope—you must help me to hope—to fancy there may yet be a silver lining to the cloud. If I did not have some hope to cling to, I could not live. I cannot live always without him, without my boy. I *must* some day hear the sound of his voice, and look upon his dear bright face again; I must, I must! No one could bear such hunger as mine for ever—no one. See now how weak I am. I, whom you thought so strong, see what a poor fond fool I am at heart—I, who try to put such a brave face on things!"

The strong broken down, the brave letting us catch a glimpse of the wound that has bled and ached so long, what more piteous sight can earth give to us? All the whinings of all the cowards in the world do not touch us as these things do. How should they?

When Lady Peyton next spoke it was in a hushed and dreamy voice—

"I hope that this woman whom he has married loves him dearly, dearly, so that she can make up to him for the rest. He must love her very dearly to have married her when there was so much to give up. If she makes him happy, I will say 'God bless her!' whatever she may be. I wish I could see her, but that I know cannot be yet. I try to fancy her, to paint her in the darkness as I lie awake at nights. If she is so dear to him, my Cyril, she must be dear to me."

"Cyril has not written—again?" said the Rector tentatively.

"His own letter was sent back to him, together with a copy of the family register in the big Bible, showing his name blotted out. How could he write again?"

"But to you?"

"He wrote once. I never saw his letter; it was burnt. Ah! do not ask me—it was like seeing something murdered. I should not have been surprised if it had cried out as the flame curled above it."

Then she came close up to him and laid her hand upon his arm, looking up with strained eyes that were growing a little wild into his pitying face.

"Mr. Darling," she said, "I have never spoken to any one like this. I have locked my sorrow in my own breast and let it heat and burn, heat and burn; but now my speech seems like a torrent that will not be stayed. You are God's minister, and to you all is

sacred, most of all—most of all—a mother's
grief. Though my eyes are dry, my heart
weeps tears of blood night and day—night
and day. Bear with me. Have pity on me,
for I have lost the desire of my eyes. Nay,
do not grieve so for me, do not look so sad.
I must be able to bear it, since God calls upon
me to do so. Perhaps it is true what he, my
husband, says. I have made an idol, and
all this is my chastisement. You turn away
from me. You think it true—you hate and
despise me—you think it true!"

"No; by the God whose minister I am I
do not think it true! Which of us may dare
to climb up into the judgment throne and
put words into the mouth of God? Take
comfort, poor sad heart. He who felt so
deeply for the divine mother's sorrow feels
for you. Somehow, somewhere, I know not
how or where—He will give you back your
boy. Meanwhile rest your care upon Him
who careth for you; wait and hope."

The flood-gates were loosened, the tears
were streaming down her face, her lips moved

as she gazed up to the sky that was paling to eventide.

"Somehow, somewhere—yes," she said at last. "I must think of those words; I must wait; I must hope. And you, you will send him my heart—my heart? He will understand."

A few moments later and Lady Peyton passed out to her carriage on the Rector's arm. Her long veil fell over her face in heavy folds, but he felt the glory of her eyes, lit up with a new peace and joy.

With bent head and pale face he returned to his study, carefully packed the ruby heart, and bidding Alison tell her mother he was going down to the village, was soon *en route* to the post-office. Amid the wondering looks of the post-mistress and her daughter at the ways of the gentlefolks in thinking nothing of double and treble postage if they had a whim to gratify, the pretty bauble was sent upon its errand of love, and the Rector set off homewards.

The light was dying overhead, but behind

the firs a glow still lingered, and the noble
spire of the old church stood out in grand
relief.

It was the ringers' practice-night, and as
the Rector passed, the sweet-voiced chimes
began to drop into the grey-gold shadowy
eventide.    To his ears they sounded as a
message of hope and love.

He stood a moment looking up at the high-
arched windows that shone with a faint reflection from the light in the western sky,
and the thoughts of his heart were as prayers
winging their flight heavenwards.

The leaves on the tall lindens by the
Rectory gates had grown golden and dropped
onto the trim paths in little wind-fluttered
heaps, thereby causing the handy-man, Maister
Straw, many deep searchings of spirit.

"I wish they hadna such untidylike ways,
Miss Alison," he said, shading his eyes with
his hand the better to look up and reproach
the few stragglers left; "or 'ud mak' up their
moinds to come down slick all at onc't.    I

reckon they think I'm paid, an' guv' my dinner Sundays, for now't else bo' to sweep them oop just when they've a moind to fall. T' missus she canna abear a litter, an' what can I do wi' the loikes o' them, never knowin' their own moinds two days together? It's onreasonable, Miss Alison, that's what it is," continued Jonathan, deeply aggrieved, as one perverse leaf came fluttering down right on his nose. "There's a deal of unreasonable things in natur', and things as 'ud ha' been reg'lated very different if I'd had a hand in 'em."

"Mamma always says how beautifully neat you keep the garden, Jonathan," said Alison gravely, though her eyes had a glint of the old twinkle in them.

"That's her politeness, Miss Alison," with a smirk. "Lord, she wouldn't hurt the feelins of a snail, wouldn't the missis; an' when I kill one o' them dratted slugs I allers takes a glance round to make sure she isn't within sight. It's fine to see her a pullin' up again, as you may say, after that bad turn as she took when the news come of Maister Cyril havin' married a black heathen mulotter as worships blocks o' stone by the roadside, and sacrifices to Baal and all such. It wur no wonder it give her a turn, for he wur a sightly young gentleman and no mistake, wur Maister Cyril. It made all Scarsdale squirmy-like, an' Mother Bond sat in her doorway laughin' an' huggin' of hersel' for three days after the news come. They do say that if Maister Cyril brought his idol-worshipper to the Old Hall the big gates would be shut in's face. Bo' happen the fayther's anger is cooled a bit now, like a pot as boils over and so puts t' foire out, for it's—let me see—it's three months an' more sin' the news came, bean't it, miss?"

"Yes; nearly four," said Alison hastily changing the subject by putting in a prompt word or two as to the shocking disposition of the last addition among the pigeons.

The sinner in question was very beautiful, as alas! many sinners are; indeed, he was a marvel, with a tail that rested on the top of

his head as he minced on tiptoe, like a fop
of the olden time.

Alison, followed respectfully by Jonathan,
stepped across to the pigeon-cotes, and sure
enough there was the faulty one, strutting
and pouting himself out, and overturning
into mid-air any inspiring fellow-pigeon who
ventured to sun himself upon the ledge.

"Did yo' ever see the loike?" cried
Jonathan. "He's loike Solomon in all his
glory, he is, and no better a man neither. I
reckon we'll have to make a pie-pigeon of
him, Miss Alison, if he don't get religion and
tone hissel' down a bit."

They were both watching the pretty warfare
waged up so high in the faint autumn sunshine, when the Rector came up from the
gate.

"Papa," said Alison; then she turned
and looked at him, and fell back a pace where
she stood.

"Papa, papa—what is it?"

But the Rector still kept silence, and she
heard his breath come heavily.

She was clinging to his arm, while Jonathan stood by wide-eyed, clutching his hat, and in mortal fear lest something had happened to " the missis," when at last he spoke :—

"Cyril Peyton is dead, and the boy Danny too. There has been some terrible accident out there."

For a moment the girl stood rigid. Then a flash dawned in her eyes, a rush of burning colour dyed her cheek.

"Papa, I will go to her; I will go to Cyril's mother. She has no one. I will not be denied. It will kill her if she has to bear it all alone."

# CHAPTER V.

ABOUT this time a ghastly and horrible adventure befell Pilkington and Master Straw—an adventure that for years to come was looked upon as a notable event in Scarsdale, and much spoken of over fires at Christmas-tide and All Hallow E'en, and other festivals upon which friends and families take to assembling themselves together for social purposes.

It will be remembered that Pilkington was the lawful apparitor of Scarsdale church; Jonathan Straw the amateur who thrust himself in, and extended the ægis of his protection over the helpless curates against her to whom nothing is sacred—the clergywoman or huntress of the black cloth. In this particular Jonathan's occupation was just now, like Othello's, gone, as was also that of the

clergywomen, to whom Sunday appeared a
day flat, dull, stale, and unprofitable, as compared with those blessed Sabbaths when dear
Mr. Westerton held sweet converse with them
in the Meadows after service, that sacred flute,
his voice, playing among the reeds and the
loosestrife, and Sophonia was not.

The result of there being no "lions in the
path" nowadays was that Jonathan obtruded
himself less into Pilkington's natural preserve,
the vestry; the result of this forbearance on
Jonathan's part was a pleasant friendliness
between the two worthy men; the result of
the friendliness, a wander through mead and
field one misty autumn evening when the sun
was low. Indeed, before the walk was ended
he went down altogether, yet the red light
lingered, and the two men, having visited a
common friend at some distance on a matter
of business, walked all the quicker homewards
for a suspicion of frost in the air, shown by
the ring of their feet on the ground. The mill
had stopped for the day, and stood all white
and weird, with the drip, drip, drip of the rest-

ing wheel sounding clear, and the weir-pool above like a dark mirror in the gloaming.

All at once the men stood still. They had turned the corner, and there, some little way off, perched upon a gate, with its elbows resting on its knees and its chin upon its folded hands, was a little figure, familiar enough to both.

"Why, it's Danny!" cried Maister Straw.

"No other," answered Pilkington, "and whatever has he bin about? He's all of a drip, and his eyes have a queer stare, mate, hanna they? Has he fell i' the millpond? and why the tarnation don't he go home to Mother Bond? She'll be out o' her head wi' joy at t' soight on him."

So they called, "Danny! Danny!" but the little figure never moved, did not even turn its head.

A watery moon was now shimmering above, and the misty light fell full upon the creature's upturned face, upon the short dank curls clinging to the pale brow, upon the blue eyes wide and staring, upon a dark red stripe down the legs of his trousers, and upon a full white-bosomed shirt that looked as if it had been newly wrung out of water.

"He's grown proud, has Danny," said Jonathan, "living among them dratted furriners. But see, mate, we'll circumvent him, and come up behind him, and give him a hearty slap and a hearty grip; for I'm glad to see the boy home again, danged if I bean't!"

They slipped over a fence and through a dew-gemmed meadow, and came up on the other side the gate.

But there was no Danny there.

Pilkington passed his hand along the uppermost bar to convince himself.

"He's run off to Mother Bond's," said he, albeit he had a questioning look in his eye as he turned to his companion.

"I hope it weren't Thomas Hancox's red cow a-looking through the bars as we saw, after all," he said, with an uneasy laugh.

"No fear," replied the other. "I saw it as plain as I see yo' a-standin' theer fornenst me."

Then they set off for Mother Bond's.

Doubtless they would find the boy Danny there. If not, they would warn the old woman that what she had watched for so long had come at last, and was on its way to her even now.

" If so be as the good-for-nowt ain't theer, we's say nothing of him being all a-drip, for that might fright her ; and when she's skeart she's apt to be nasty," said Jonathan.

"Oh, he's there, safe enough," said Pilkington.

But when they reached Mother Bond's tumble-down abode a certain hesitation was noticeable in each. No light burned in the small patched window, and a ragged old hen which kept company with Mother Bond was huddled up against the closed door, and made a feeble clucking as she saw them.

It was Jonathan who pressed the latch and shoved the door as far open as it would go— Jonathan who started back as a dull, heavy thud came against the panels, and the door closed again of itself.

"Whatever's ado?" he said.   "I canna get the place open."

Then Pilkington tried, shoving hard against some soft and yet persistent resistance from within.

Once inside, followed by the ruffled and clucking hen, the two men looked round, but in the feeble dying light could distinguish nothing more than the faint outline of what looked like a sack hanging behind the door.

"Hast 'er got a light?" said Jonathan.

Pilkington brought out a tin box of matches, and struck one upon his rough corduroy trousers-leg.

Up started shadows in every corner, and they saw the old hen cowering among the cinders on the cold and fireless hearth.   They saw more than that: they saw old Mother Bond, stiff and dead, hanging by the neck from an iron hook behind the door.

With a wild scream, Pilkington fled out into the garden; but Master Straw, made of sterner stuff, and now and again called upon to act as assistant-constable, lit a guttered candle that stood in a battered candlestick on the high, narrow mantle-shelf, and stepped boldly up to the swinging-horror that was once a living woman.

Pilkington, who was by this time skulking and peeping in, at this summoned up some sort of quality that he called by the name of courage, and stole a-tiptoe to his friend's side.

And the ghastly thing before them swayed slowly from side to side like a horrible pendulum.

"Keep it still; canna yo' keep it still?" whimpered Pilkington; "it makes it worse to see it move that way. O Lord, O Lord! I'll never be my own man agen, I knows I won't."

But of these maunderings, Master Straw took no heed.

He lifted the wisp of elf-locks that had fallen over the face; he held the flickering candle close to the half-closed eyes, the gaping, discoloured mouth; he touched the stiffened outstretched hands that hung among the bundle of rags that Mother Bond had been wont to call her clothes.

Then he spoke—

" Dead," he said, " dead as dead, stiff and cold this hour or more."

" Ay, ay," said poor Pilkington. " Come away, neighbour, come away."

But Jonathan would not hurry. He cut down the poor shrivelled body, severed the rope about the skinny throat and laid all that was left of Mother Bond upon the shabby settle in the corner, constraining Pilkington to assist in the gruesome work though his teeth chattered like castanets, and he shook as with the palsy. Then Jonathan picked up the poor draggled hen and tucked it under his arm, blew out the candle and set it in its place, and following his companion out, closed to the door.

" What about the boy Danny ? " said Pilkington as the two made for the village.

" It wur a boggart as we saw," replied the other, " an' nowt else."

Pilkington squirmed in the road. Was it

not enough that he must see a dead woman hanging from a hook, but that he must also see a boggart—a ghost—a spirit?

How could any one ever expect he should be his own man again if these things were so?

It may be fairly said that the red glow of the cosy window at the Golden Crown was welcome to both men. Certain it is that they precipitated themselves, hen and all, helter-skelter into that safe retreat, and then and there to the assembled company told their marvellous terrible tale, amid a clatter of tongues such as might well recall the days of Babel's Tower.

"It wur a boggart," cried the sturdy farmer whom we ken of yore; "it wur a boggart and nowt else; for the boy Danny's dead—drownded dead, an' Maister Cyril too. The news come but a while ago, an' t' Rector's daughter is oop at t' Ould Hall wi' my Leddy, who's stricken into a great sickness wi' grief an' sorrow, same as Rachel who we hear of in the olden time."

At this Pilkington fell into a chair, and

the buxom landlady, with much presence of mind, drew a glass of the best Scotch and poured it down his willing throat.

The farmer, encouraged by the effects of his own eloquence, went on rapidly, the rest listening intently.

"He died a gran' death, did Danny. There wur a great storm arose in those parts, an' a ship was sinkin' wi' all hands, and Danny he went along wi' the rest to try an' save some on 'em, but he never came back alive; and he's got hisself in the papers, an' I tell yo' he made a gran' end, did Danny."

"He wur all a-drip," said Maister Straw, speaking in a dazed and dreamy fashion, and looking hard at nothing, "all a-drip—all a-drip!"

After which there was an awed silence, which the tripod took to be a likely opening.

Up he got, wavering on his three legs.

"Our Elizabeth Ann she saw a boggart onc't; it wur in the back cellar, and it took the form of a monstrous black pig."

But at this stage they shouted to him to

"howd his noise," and some one giving him a friendly shove, he fell into a mere heap of clothes in the old chair behind the door.

Then a messenger was sent to inform the constable of how matters stood up at Mother Bond's, and another to warn the doctor, the while Pilkington, with tears in his eyes besought Maister Straw to see him safe home— a request to which that champion assented. But their progress was slow, for every now and then Pilkington came to a halt, and clung on to his companion, saying what an awful sight it was to see the white-faced boggart "settin' on the rail an' lookin' so solemn-like at t' mune."

"I reckon you'd look solemn-like if you was a boggart," said Jonathan. "You know it canna be a cheerful thing to be a boggart settin' on a rail and scaring honest folks out o' their wits. That one scared Mother Bond to her death, I'm danged if he didna! Happen he squirmed in at t' winder."

But at this Pilkington showed signs of becoming convulsive, so Jonathan desisted.

But he could not get Danny out of his mind.

"He died a gran' death, he made a gran' end, did Danny; and now he's where the weary cease from troublin' an' the wicked are at rest.   Ay, ay, he'd need to be theer—he'd need to be at rest to do ony mortal good, would Danny.   He wur a tricky one, he wur, and it 'ull tak' the good Lord all his time to make owt o' Danny Spool; but we mun ha' faith—we mun ha' faith."

That was Danny's epitaph at home.

# CHAPTER VI.

## "THOSE WHOSE WORK IS DONE."

SHE told herself that Cyril was dead, that she should never see his bright face again, never meet the glance of his loving eyes, never see the winsome smile upon his lips, never hear the happy music of his voice, never meet him, never greet him; she told herself that the face she loved was hidden by the coffin-lid, that the feet, ever so ready to bring him to her, lay cold and still, the hands that had grasped hers so tenderly were folded across the stirless breast.

She told herself these things over and over again, but she always seemed to be telling the story of some one else, not of Cyril, and to some one else, not to his mother, Marion, Lady Peyton.

Fight as she would, she could not put

aside this sense of the unreality of things around her, herself included. Even her memory seemed to fail. She could not call up, with the vividness of the past, those pretty memories of her darling's boyish days in which she had so often found comfort. To dwell upon them was to pursue what evaded her, torturing her with indistinct colouring and blurred outlines. She had lost everything. The present and the past were both alike arid and desolate. She was beyond wonder, and took the unaccustomed presence of the Rector's daughter as a thing of course. As to Alison, her tendance of the suffering woman was an outlet to the pent-up tenderness of years. If some exquisite content in what seemed to her the highest privilege possible lurked beneath the sorrow of the hour, and was unconsciously to herself linked by golden chains to the short sweet day of her love for Lance, who can wonder? If Lady Peyton was to her not alone one whom she had long loved and honoured from afar, but also—that most sacred and precious

thing to a woman's heart—the mother of the
man she loved, who could find in their hearts
to blame her?

Even Mrs. Dutton was satisfied with the
devotion and care Alison gave to her dear
Lady; and if Mrs. Dutton was satisfied, then
might all the world be well content.

Truly it would have been hard even for the
most exacting to find fault with Alison.

Like some loving shadow, she was ever at
hand to help and tend the grief-stricken
mother, yet so silent and unobtrusive in her
sympathy, that it seemed nothing strange to
those around her to see her in their midst,
and turn to her for help and guidance.

Lance and his wife were abroad, whither
they had gone for Lady Jane's health, which,
never robust, failed altogether after the loss
of her baby son; but when the news of
Cyril's death came, she, with characteristic
unselfishness, urged her husband to hurry to
Gibraltar and see what arrangements could
be made for the poor young widowed bride.
The Lady Jane had been deeply troubled

by the marriage her husband's brother had made, but wrote so tenderly and sympathetically to Cyril at the time, that the poor boy—he was little more at heart, no matter what his years—wept tears of thankfulness over the letter; and Juanita, with all the passionate impulsiveness of her Southern nature, kissed the paper and pressed it to her heart.

"It is so terrible that your father should have cast poor Cyril aside like this," said Lady Jane to her husband, "that the boy should have died alienated from all dearest to him. And think—think, dear Lance, how he must have loved her to risk everything—to say, as he did to you, that he would do it twice over if the thing had to be lived through again; think of the piteous story of the ruby heart, and how he wrote, 'I knew so well all it meant, how it came to me as her heart, her dear true heart, with its loving message;' think of all these things, and now fancy the girl's desolation, she who has had no sin towards any of us save loving our bright Cyril too well. You see I talk as if I had known him quite well, as indeed I have—indeed I have, in my heart, Lance. And now, go to her, dear husband. I am sure I am stronger to-day. See, I can stand alone; I can get across the room. There! you will go, will you not! O Lance, Lance! think what it would be if I lost you! My darling, my darling! should I not stand sorely in need of comfort?"

She was kneeling by his side, her arms about his neck, her face against his breast.

He was strange, wayward, moody, sometimes harsh, but he was her own, her husband, not another.

Doubtless Lance felt some shame as he put his arm gently round her and led her back to her couch. Such outbreaks of tenderness on her part were rare, and he—well, he loved her, reverenced her; but the sweet passion of the rose-garden had died out in his heart when he parted with Alison Darling, and the light could be illumined no more.

Saddest of all human stories is that of the

love which is given without stint, and meets
no adequate return in this world ; but

"Is human love the gift of human will?"

Nay, rather is it a flower that springs spon-
taneously from the heart, and may be gathered
by one hand alone.

Crushed by the news of his brother's death
—the news that fell so heavily, since it called
forth a thousand little stings of remorse for
things that might have been, and now could
never be—Lance was conscious of a ray of
comfort when an ill-spelled yet most tender
and sweet letter from Mrs. Dutton told him
how the Rector's young lady was with her
ladyship, mostly holding her sorrowful hand,
and following her about, together with Hound,
and singing soft-like in the twilight evenings,
and the Rector himself was often there, and
spoke high and holy words.

Then the letter went on to say—

"But my Lady does not notice much ; a
great stillness is on her since she knew that
Master Cyril would come no more."

"A great stillness—a great stillness." The words seemed to ring in his ears, and he groaned aloud.

A stillness that nothing could break—a silence that nothing could fill.

Yes; he knew how it was; he had long since read the story of his mother's life with eyes that saw clearly at last. With husband and sons, enough one would think to fill the heart of any woman, one only of the three had ever brought the sunshine of light and joy into her life, and now that one was gone. As the sunflower turns to the sun, so had she turned towards the one radiance of whose warmth she was conscious, and now blackness and a thick darkness were for her over all the world.

As Alison and the faithful Dutton watched her, it seemed to their loving eyes as though the sorrowing mother had passed away to some distant bourne, where she was out of reach alike of touch and hearing.

Stretch out their tender hands as they might, they could not reach her; speak in

ever so loving a voice, the words seemed to
fall upon ears that heard not.

A steady heart-broken defiance looked at
them out of her mournful eyes; when they
spoke to her of her boy, his winning ways,
and his fond love for herself, when they told
the old, old stories, in the hope that tears
would come and mercifully soften that awful
fixed gaze, she only passed her hand across
her forehead and said—

"I do not remember."

It seemed that this stupor, this deadness
to all around her, had come upon her in the
hour when Sir Marmaduke, with words that
hit her like blows, told her that her son
Cyril was dead.

That mighty awful news hushed all the
rest of earth's voices, deadened and stunned
the poor brain that with laboured effort took
it in.

Then Alison came, low-voiced, soft-footed,
with few words, and only a gentle clasping
of the cold hand, or, at most, a soft touch of
the lips upon the listless fingers.

If Alison had lived at the Old Hall all her life, Lady Peyton could not have shown less surprise at her constant presence there; she even missed her if she went away for a while, looking restlessly at the door and wandering to the window.

As for Sir Marmaduke, he spent his time mostly locked in his own special room.

When a man has hated and thwarted any one all his life, there is something overpowering even to the most hardened in the swift flash that cuts the young life short, and places it for ever beyond the power of hate or anger, " safe-garnered up with God."

What memories of the past haunted that locked chamber? What thoughts burnt and stung the heart of the man who there kept solitary vigil? Did the sunlight streaming through the high window catch the gleam of a child's golden hair? Did a little figure come to the casement and beat with a tiny finger on the diamond panes? Did a boy in all the glow and glory of his youth and beauty stand there in the shadowy gloaming, with the glint of the firelight on his lovely troubled face ?

Did a voice tremble through the shadows :— "Father, why were you always so hard upon me ?"

God help those of us who are haunted by such pale reproachful ghosts as these torturing remorseful memories, that, taking weird shape and form, look at us with sad reproachful eyes, and will not be put aside !

To love and lose is hard enough, but to suffer the bitter pangs of self-reproach when our dead are taken from us, that is to cry with Cain, "My punishment is greater than I can bear."

In Dutton's faithful breast were locked many sad and terrible records of life at the Old Hall. Perhaps no one else could have told the full extent of the sorrows and trials of Marion, Lady Peyton ; no one else furnish the details of miserable petty tyranny on the one hand, and heroic patience and endurance on the other. But Dutton's lips were sealed.

Every smallest thing concerning her beloved mistress was sacred in her eyes; and not even to Miss Alison, gentle and tender as she was in her ministrations to the stricken lady, would the faithful servitor have spoken of the secrets of that prison-house, the old manor, with the pine-woods clustering on the hill behind.

Presently began to come to hand records of Cyril Peyton's death, and to Sir Marmaduke even these records held within them the root of bitterness, for each letter in its turn, the Colonel's, Captain Gildea's, Mrs. Kershaw's (this last blurred and blotted with tears), was as a stave of the same melody—how every one loved him, how every one missed his bright presence, how the men of his company insisted upon putting up a small white marble cross over his grave as a tribute from themselves to his dear and honoured memory. He was mourned as a sweet-souled, clean-hearted, manly young fellow is mourned in the regiment to which he belongs, and there is no sorrow more true, more lasting, or more sincere.

A regiment becomes nothing but one big united family in the presence of a common sorrow. All petty spites, feuds, and jealousies are forgotten, and merged in the general grief; all distinctions of class and rank go for nothing, as the cord of sorrow binds heart to heart and man to man. From the Colonel himself down to the most infinitesimal drummer-boy all are sympathetic, all united in one bond, as the drums roll and the fifes shriek, and the volley is fired over the open grave.

The story of the tragedy was this. A storm had raged about the Rock, a storm sudden, unlooked for, beyond precedent, and a ship was drifting, drifting on to death. With bare rigging, now dipping into the raging sea, now swinging aloft, showing like a dark web against the purple wrack, on she came. Those who could face the fury of the gale gathered on the shore, the foreign boatmen, praying and crossing themselves, gesticulating and screaming; the Englishmen, as became their kind, silent and awed, but showing little outward emotion.

Suddenly above the shriek of the wind and the mighty roar of the surf rose a cry—a shout as of one man from many throats.

On the swaying shuddering ropes were seen clinging or lashed—no one could say which —cowering forms of men fighting a bitter fight for life.

Then came hurrying to and fro, little crowds forming here and there, and then drifting apart; men gathering in knots, one here, one there, seeming to take the lead.

The sudden glare of a lantern lit up Cyril Peyton's face, bright, eager, resolute, and Gildea, standing near, turned and looked. He was glad afterwards that he had been given that last glance, that last smile, as the boy went to his noble death.

Three boats put off, all manned by English soldiers and sailors. Beating about in the boiling surf, gaining a yard or two with a fearful expenditure of labour, and, with arms and oars alike quivering with the strain, gaining yet a yard or two more—this was the work these men had to face.

Of the boat in which Cyril found himself, clutching the tiller as though he himself were drowning, and that one bar of wood his only hope and stay, we must now tell the story.

Scarcely had it ploughed its way even across the white fringe of the shore-breakers when from under the meagre shelter of the gunwale crawled forth a diminutive figure in small regulation trousers and shirt, and the men shouted out in the teeth of the wind—

" Why, it's Drummer Danny ! "

" I thought the Chief gave orders that no boys were to be allowed out to-night," shouted Wobbler, seated next a brawny tar, and labouring at an oar with the best, and with all his affectations laid aside like a discarded garment.

Cyril shook his head.

Danny was beyond orders, and his delinquencies were too often winked at by the non-coms., as was well known in the 97th.

In a lull of the storm Danny crept to Cyril's side.

"I was allers a stowaway, sir," he said; "and I couldna but foller on to yo', Maister Cyril—I allers did, yo' know."

It sounded like a voice from the dead past to Cyril's ears, but the lapse of discipline in the use of the old-time name escaped censure in this supreme hour, and Danny, with a rope round his middle, and his eyes glaring through the haze like a ferret's, grasped the edge of the boat like a vice, and stared unblinkingly at the tossing rigging with its load of human lives.

"I can swim like a fish, sir," he said, when he showed the rope, not without some pride. "Yo' can toss me overboard when yo' like, and I reckon I'll reach her, and stick too; but we must get nigher first, Maister Cyril."

The men would have stared at this, could they have spared any thought or notice at such a moment, but every nerve and sense was strained.

When the awful story of that night came to be told, few could remember what happened after that.

There was a crash, and some part of the wreck drifted on to them with terrific force, resistless as that of a battering-ram; a crash, too, against the gunwale of their own boat; a leap, a lurch, as the tiller sprang from a stricken hand, and Cyril Peyton's place was empty.

Then came the swell of a mighty wave, and the light from a lantern held high above the flood glinted on a white face drifting across the green mirror of the mounting water; then a cry, the swift passage of a body through the air, the green wall of water smitten, a shout to "keep the rope taut," and the wave crested and broke, half filling the boat with water, and making her shudder in every plank as she fell in the trough of the sea.

They held the rope, raised the light, and drew in Danny, lifting him tenderly in their strong arms. But either the boy's life had been beaten out of him by the resistless force of the wave, or he had struck against some floating wreckage.

The pet of the regiment lay lifeless across the knees of a big drummer, who called him "Danny boy," and bade him "keep up his heart," and "never say die," all in vain, and presently began to hug him up and whimper over him, rolling him in the coat taken from his own shoulders. A watery moon showed for a moment through the scud as the boat was driven on to the shore, and touched the boy's dead face with a tearful radiance.

"Look at the eyes of him," said the drummer with a sob. "Some on you cover 'em up; don't let 'em stare and stare that way. Oh, Danny, my boy, we'll never see the likes of you agin for the double-shuffle an' the step-dance. Sure an' it wasna steppin' at all, for your feet fluttered like a pair o' burrds, so as none could tell where they was and where they wasn't. Ochone! but it was the rale broth of a boy you was, Drummer Danny!"

This was Danny's epitaph in his regiment.

And it may be said of him that he had been consistent in all things. He had always "follered on to Maister Cyril" as best as he was able.

One of the other boats picked up the body of Lieutenant Peyton. There was a ragged gash just where the hair grew so finely on the temple, and death had set its seal upon the face which to look upon had been to love. Gone were the winning smile and the bright boyish gleam of the soft brown eyes, but the face was noble in its repose, and the young life had been laid down in a noble cause.

The third boat had reached the wreck and rescued the men from the rigging; but these lives had been redeemed at a mighty cost, and the 97th bitterly mourned its dead.

It fell to the lot of Captain Gildea to go and tell Cyril's young wife that she was a widow.

All of us who have done much foreign service well know the sensation and thrill in a regiment when one of its officers makes a *mésalliance;* the unspeakable wrath of the

Colonel commanding; the united efforts of the rest to turn the sinner from his fell purpose; the absolute uselessness of all these efforts; and then the isolation of the undesirable bride, the agitated discussions of the ladies of the regiment as to whether she is to be called upon or not, the disquieting nature of the whole affair, the angry letters of the misguided man's " people," which fan the Colonel's wrath to furious flames; finally, the acceptance of the inevitable, since marriage, like death, is a thing that can neither be got over nor set aside, and the dying away of violent disputations before the advent of some newer wonder.

In poor Cyril's case all this had been gone through save the last stage, for he had announced that Mrs. Cyril Peyton wished to live still in strict seclusion, consequently curiosity about and interest in her did not die a natural death, all the less so since one or two who had caught a glimpse of Juanita vowed her beauty was a thing to dazzle your eyes.

It may be said that Gildea, generous and impulsive, with the generosity and impulsiveness of his nation, volunteered to go as the bearer of evil tidings, and the Wobbler—well, the Wobbler vowed he would not desert a comrade in the day of trial; but never had he better deserved his sobriquet than when the two set out for the grey-walled villa.

The face of Dorrington, as seen at the gate of the officers' quarters, had not made things better for the Wobbler—Dorrington, in regimental trousers, with a tunic slung over his arm, and a forage cap on his dark close-cropped head, carrying some batman's clothes, to be laid by with other "effects" of Lieutenant Peyton, deceased, to be presently disposed of.

"I'm a-going back to the ranks, sir," said Dorrington, saluting; "I'm not to serve no other master, now *he's* gone."

The man's face twitched, and though he passed the sleeve of his shirt across his eyes, the tears could not be hidden. The Wobbler

would like to have said some words of comfort, but was past speaking, and could only
shake his head and screw his glass into his
eye. Were there not things that had been
known only to himself and the man who
now lay dead with the Union Jack across
his pillow?—times when the Wobbler had
needed a friendly hand, and never failed to
find it—times of which the memory might
well now rise up and choke him?

Silent indeed was the walk to the villa.
Gildea, pale but determined, and with a sort
of blind trust that words would be given
to him when the moment of need should
come; the Wobbler, distinctly spasmodic, and
saying to himself that he would rather row
through all the surfs on all the coasts to
rescue any number of drowning men you like
to name, than have to blight a woman's life
with the news he now carried.

The door in the wall reached, it was Gildea
who pulled the chain. Then he turned to
his companion and said—

"I think you had better wait out here.

This is a job a man can do best single-handed. If I find I need you I will come for you."

The Wobbler nodded, and at that moment the door opened like a chink, and Maritana's withered old face appeared at the aperture.

"Not here—the signor not here," she said, defending her citadel according to her lights.

But Gildea was past her like a flash, and, hurrying wildly after him, she left that usually well-guarded portal ajar.

In thinking over things afterwards, it appeared to the man who waited that Gildea was from three to four hours engaged in breaking the news of poor Peyton's death to the young widow. When he consulted his watch, he found it must have been about twenty or five-and-twenty minutes.

Once the Wobbler thought he heard a bitter wailing cry, and he—the man who would have faced the enemy's guns or fixed bayonets without a flinch—put his fingers in his ears, and walked quickly along the dusty road for some distance.

Then Gildea came out, and after one glance

at his face, his companion dared not ask him any question. In silence, even as they had come, the two set off homewards to the fortress; then Gildea said—

"Thank you, old fellow, for having kept me company," and turned towards the Kershaws' place, leaving the other to wend his way to the barracks.

Five or six days later, Mr. Launcelot Peyton reached Gibraltar, and when he, together with Major and Mrs. Kershaw, visited the walled-in house, they found it, so to say, swept and garnished.

A little round tambour-frame lay on the step of the vestibule, and a black lace-edged apron hung over a narrow high-backed chair; but of any other sign of female personality there was none.

A tall, black-robed, quiet-faced priest had opened the garden door to the visitors, bowing with a grace that might well have become a courtier.

"I am Mr. Cyril Peyton's brother. Can I see his wife?"

"Ah!" said the priest, "it is so sad, so sad that he is dead," and he spread his hands out as though pronouncing a benediction on the company before him.

"But his wife—his wife?" urged Lance, his dark face lighting up with quick anger at what he looked upon as shuffling.

"A—h!" (this with a slow shake of the head and a shrug of the shoulders that made Major Kershaw feel murderous), "she is a . . . . way."

"Away! where?" said Lance sternly.

"How can I know all things?" asked the other, leading the way into the vestibule. "I can say only what I know. I learn the Engleesh from Juanita, and I tell you she is away."

"Where's her blackguard of an uncle?" said Major Kershaw, with an air as though he were questioning an orderly-room culprit.

"Stanley! Stanley!" said Mrs. Kershaw, but Stanley was apparently deaf for the nonce.

"Ah! yes, it is so," said the priest;

"that is one of your Engleesh regiments, the Bla-gi-ards! I have heard tell of it; but Pedro Montalba had nothing at all to do with that Engleesh regiment. He was a very good poor man, but he fell in great temptation, and he is die in preeson."

"Now, you see, Stanley, it is no use interfering; he cannot understand you."

"I'm not so sure of that," said the irate Major. "I think it's all just his damned impudence."

The good father was not at all disturbed by the sound of the expletive.

The English were made so; what would you? He stood by, patient and courteous, with a gentle persistence in giving no information whatever, that at last drove the two men to a frenzy; while as for Mrs. Kershaw, she had to stand and look out through the little, square, leaf-wreathed window we know of, to hide the tears that came creeping down her cheeks.

It was all so silent and so desolate! The sunshine kissing the perfumed flowers, the

amber fruit peeping through the brilliant green
of the orange-leaves—what a mockery it all
seemed !

The scene of the sweet and passionate love
idyll—the rooms that had been melodious
with the sound of the mandoline and the
music of Juanita's voice, that had been
merry with Cyril's laughter—now empty and
silent !

Ah ! heaven, how glad she was that she had
been kind to the boy—the boy whom little
Alice had loved so dearly ; how glad she was
that she had told him she would come and
visit his bride ; that she had let him chatter
to her of the life at the little villa ; of his
joy, his pride, his sweet content in that—the
Eden of his heart !

How glad we all are, my friends, when
some one we love is taken from us, that
little kindnesses were not left undone—the
little comforts not withheld !

After a long and wearying lingering in
Cyril's desolate home, Lance and the others
had to turn their steps homewards, with no

better information than that first offered to
them—

"She is a . . . . way."

Nor did any further news of the missing
bride ever reach the fortress.

Like a breath upon a mirror had she
passed, soon to be forgotten in the whirl and
change of military life; but when the 97th
got the route, and sailed away from the
great fortress, Mary Kershaw, as the trooper
sped upon its way, gave loving and regretful
thought to the brave young soldier lying
in his grave, and the girl who had gone, no
one knew whither, with her broken, sorrowing
heart.

She did not forget Drummer Danny either;
and it was said on board more than once
among the men that the step-dancers who
tried their skill for the evening's diversion
" couldn't hold a candle to the lad we left
behind us, and, compared to him, were mere
bunglers at the trick."

"Papa," said Alison, her lips quivering,

her sweet eyes glistening with starting tears,
"will she be always like this—always? Will
she never remember, and weep the hard gaze
from her eyes?"

"My darling," he said, touching her hair
caressingly, "we must wait and hope; she is
in our Father's hands. Oh, my dear, what
can you do more than you are doing? Wait
and pray. I think," said the Rector, with the
quaint simplicity of one who discovers a truth
for the first time, "that there is no harder
work in life than waiting."

They had not much longer to wait; and,
as is so often the case with prayers that,
rising from troubled hearts, know not what
they ask, the answer came in a way but little
thought of. Lady Peyton was alone in the
library, and some memory of her boy's childish
days must have unsealed the fountain of her
tears; for, as her husband entered, she turned
towards him a face bedewed with tears—eyes
pleading, full of the pain and anguish of a
mother's sorrow.

"Marmaduke," she said, stretching out her

hand to him, forgetful for the moment of the coldness of years, the estrangement of these latter days, "do you remember, when Cyril left us, how we caught our last glimpse of him there—just at the turn of the drive ?"

He pushed her hand aside, come close up to her, and looked sternly down upon her.

"Still harping on your idol, still undisciplined. I tell you if you had not made an idol of your boy this chastisement would not have fallen upon you. Cry aloud in sackcloth and ashes to the God you have offended ; do not whine like a whipped cur because that graceless boy——"

Sir Marmaduke got no further. His wife rose to her feet, lifted her arms high above her head in a supreme gesture of horror and despair, and with a cry in which all the anguish of the years found utterance, fell heavily forward at his feet.

The wild pealing of the library bell brought help, but when they raised her, the beautiful face was drawn and changed, the flaccid lips "babbled o' green fields," and uttered a language it was given to no man to understand. When the hour came that they stood about her dying bed, Alison nearest to her, with the dear head upon her breast, the Rector on his knees, Sir Marmaduke crouching on the couch at the foot of the bed, and Dutton—poor broken-hearted Dutton!—sobbing in an abandonment of grief, they became suddenly conscious that the dying woman was making a terrible effort to speak.

The doctor, come all the way from London, and able to do so little now he had come, spoke hurriedly to Alison—

"Raise her up."

The strong and tender arms were quick and ready.

"What is it, dear?" said Alison. "Try to tell us."

A faint flush rose to the waxen cheek; the drooping lids quivered; the labouring breast was still a moment. Then, in a voice that no one knew, came one slow sentence—

" Be—good—to— Cyril's—wife."

Upon this a silence, until Alison broke out sobbing, and with one long shuddering sigh the gracious head fell back, and Marion, Lady Peyton, was at rest for ever.

# CHAPTER VII.

## THE BANSHEE.

CHOIR-PRACTICE was over. The boys had dropped out of the church one by one, foregathering when well out of the ken of the Rector and the organist, and tripping one another up amongst the tombstones and down the steps to their hearts' content.

They had had rather a stormy time of it with Mr. Flip, the choir-leader, who absolutely refused to believe that the line of a well-known hymn—

"What though in lonely grief I sigh,"

should be bawled with all the force possible to ten growing boys, while an added solemnity had been lent to the occasion by the somewhat unwonted presence of the Rector, beating time in a portly and dignified manner with his folded *pince-nez*, and sharply down upon a lapse in time. "Like one o'clock," as the most cheeky of the choir put it, "an' fit to snap yer head off."

Inside all was light and warmth, outside the grey shadows crept among the graves, and the swinging lamp above the gate at the foot of the steep steps shone mistily; for though spring was near at hand, it had not yet wooed the crocuses from their sheltering bulbs, nor perceptibly lengthened out the days.

On the strength of a firm belief that the Rector and Miss Alison would linger to have a few words with Mr. Flip, a grand storming of the steps—enemy below, besieged above— was undertaken, with the necessary concession to possible danger that voices should be subdued, and scuffles as silently conducted as might be. All this caution was, however, rendered useless and set at naught by little Johnny Linnet tripping over a bigger boy's foot, and rolling down the disputed declivity from top to bottom.

Happily, Johnny was as round and plump as a fat partridge, so no bones were broken, but a round bump on his forehead was an excellent excuse for a bellow, and the defending and attacking forces combined to hustle him away, almost running him off his little fat legs down the hill into the village, the while Mr. Flip came out from the church, hatless and indignant, just in time to see the tail end of the flying column disappear round the turn of the road.

Mr. Flip went back into the church for his hat, then emerged, and, being a man who was always in a hurry, no matter what hour of the day you met him, "slithered" down the steps —we use a word specially invented for Mr. Flip by Jonathan Straw—and disappeared among the growing shadows. Came then the little curate, his little wife having dutifully waited for him in the porch, and now tucked under his little arm, trotted down the steps with a perky, jerky gait not unlike that of a sparrow, and so out into the shadows too. Came Pilkington with his best bow—of a

quality not to be sneezed at, mind you—to
the Rector and Miss Alison, and the keys
rattling in his hand, a noise not unwelcome
to his ears, as savouring of office, and the
consideration due from meaner minds to one
in the position of an apparitor, and he too
goes down the steps, becomes a black shadow
among the grey, and so melts. Came Mr.
Darling and Alison, lingeringly, not in a
hurry like the rest, but as though held back
by some subtle influence; as though their feet
loved to touch the sacred ground of the dear
God's Acre, where so many headstones gleamed
white amid the shadows.

"We seem to have lived such a full—nay,
I had almost said such a terrible life of late,
papa," said Alison. "I think Scarsdale has
been like a stream, quiet, almost hidden
among the tall grasses, and then suddenly to
have overflowed its banks and become a tossing turbulent river."

Unconsciously, as it seemed, they had
wandered to a spot in the churchyard where
the earth still showed fresh, and where, as

yet, no headstone bore name and date, but
where the loving hands of Alison had planted
all sweet things that keep green through
winter snows.

"Yes," said the Rector, looking down upon
the ground that was here and there just
pierced by the tips of the pale spears of the
snowdrop leaves, "yes, it has been a stormy
time, but for some the Master has hushed the
waves and said, 'Be still.'  Alison, I think of
that weary troubled heart now at rest, and
can thank God, even though her gain is our
deep loss.  My own words come back to me
as I stand here.  'Somehow, somewhere, I
know not how or when, God will give you
back your boy;' and the memory of a white
rapt face, of hands clasped so tight they
trembled with the pressure, is with me, and
I see now how my words came true.  God
has given her back her boy.  He could not
come to her; she has gone to him."

"It seems but yesterday that she was here
with us—of us; and oh, so dear!  And yet
see, papa, the snowdrops that I set when

she died are peeping up out of the brown earth."

"I shall never forget," went on the Rector, "the singing of the hymn as they bore her to her grave. I shall never hear the words again while I live without the whole scene rising up before me."

Alison's soft voice made answer thus—

> "Now the labourer's task is o'er,
>   Now the battle-day is past;
> Now upon the farther shore
>   Lands the voyager at last.
> Father, in Thy gracious keeping,
> Leave we now Thy servant sleeping."

"It was a hard task, papa, a cruel battle. It would be selfish to wish her back again, but I miss her—I miss her more than I can say. I feel like some one who has been listening to a noble strain of organ-music, and who is conscious of the ache of silence; and I think of her last words, of the dear eyes looking at us as from somewhere very far away, and I say to myself, 'How can we—*can* we be good to Cyril's wife when no one can find her?' Oh, papa, if some one only could!

We should know her, should we not? by the great ruby heart that she is sure—quite sure to have always about her neck; the jewel that said so little, and meant so much."

By this time the two had paced slowly down the steps, the Rector had carefully closed the gates, and set off, still slowly and thoughtfully, homewards.

"Everything has been and is being done," continued Mr. Darling, "to find this missing lady; but she is indeed a *fata morgana*, a shadow that none can grasp—nay, not even touch, for all trace of her seems lost."

"It was a great pity that Lady Jane's increased illness forced Lance to leave Gibraltar so soon. He might have searched out some clue or other; and I am sure—I always have been sure, I always shall be sure—that that priest (the one Lance told you about in his letter) knew where the poor soul had fled to. He's a mean, narrow-minded bigot, papa, and afraid of poor Cyril's Protestant friends. Don't tell me!"

And the fair head was tossed so that the

violets in Alison's neat little hat vibrated as though a breeze shook them.

"Hush, hush!" said the Rector, smiling, though, at this little stormy outburst. "You must judge a man from his own standpoint, not from yours. If you held that worthy man's creed, and held it sincerely, you would be narrow-minded and a bigot; in truth, I do not know what extremes you might not be driven to. There are no extremes to which a man or woman who thoroughly embraces all the dogmas of Catholicism may not be driven, since for them the end must justify the means."

"Then you think he—this priest—thought he was doing right when he hid poor Juanita from those who would have befriended her?"

"Certainly, *if* he hid her."

"Of course he did!" and again the nodding violets were shaken by the breeze.

"My dear, we do not know that he did so; we can only conjecture."

"Still, I do think, papa, it is rather hard of you to say that he was right."

"My dear, I said he thought he was right —a very different thing, if you will allow me to say so."

"Forgive me, dear" (Alison had a way of calling her father "dear" in any special moments); "I am a perfect cross-patch, I know, but I do feel bad over it all, and strange fancies come over me. I think to myself that the poor thing may be lonely, poor, a wanderer on the face of the earth. Oh, I know not what I think; and the dying voice seems to echo in my ear and in my heart, 'Be kind to Cyril's wife; be kind to Cyril's wife.'"

The last word came with a sob, and the Rector looked anxiously at his daughter.

"You are over-wrought, child," he said at last; "and, indeed, what wonder? The stoutest heart among us quailed, I think, at all the horrors that have come to pass in these strange latter times. Mother Bond's funeral took it out of me not a little, I must confess—the crowd and the hubbub, and then all the horrors of the inquest. No one can

ever call Scarsdale a monotonous place again,
Alison, can they?"

"No," said Alison, shaking her head; "I
think a little monotony would be welcome,
I do indeed: but no one feels sure, while
Sir Marmaduke goes on acting in such an
eccentric way, what may happen next."

"You mean his refusing to see any one,
and wandering about the grounds at night?"

"Papa, it is remorse that drives him,"
broke out Alison, "and remorse must be
a heavy whip. Do you remember his face
that night—the night she died? It was
like a veil being lifted, and letting one see
into the man's soul, just for a moment, as it
were."

"Poor soul!" said the Rector gently, "that
can see no beauty in Nature, no love in the
Creator, that worships some impossible devil
and calls it God, and yet sincere—sincere, I
do believe."

"What? Sincere in thinking it was right,
no matter what this devil you say he worshipped told him to do, to break that noble

heart, darken that beautiful life? No, no, no! I tell you, papa, that he is sorry now—now, when it is too late."

"It is never too late to be sorry," said the Rector.

At which Alison was silent.

Then they met Maister Straw with news issuing from every pore of his skin.

"Have yo' hearn, sir," he said, standing stock-still in the middle of the road, and mopping his brow with a handkerchief red enough to frighten all the cows in the Meadows, "have yo' hearn as Sir Marmy-dook's a-going off into furrin' parts to-morrow mornin' as ever is? There's bin a vast topsy-turvey going on at t' Owd Hall all this blessed day, an' Mistress Dutton hasna an eye left i' her yed wi' cryin'. She'll be mortial lonesome i' that big an' silent house —mortial, mortial lonesome, will Mistress Dutton. I mind her comin' there, Miss Alison. A comely wench as yo' might see i' a day's march, that were she, an' no one never thinkin' to see her raised so high as now she's clomb; but my Lady took kindly to her, and step by step she rose till she topped the lot of 'em. I was young mysel' then, Miss Alison, an' Maister Lance and Maister Cyril—God bless them!—were wee bits o' chappies wi' little sailor-hats, an', axing your pardon, Master Lance used to call you his little sweetheart. I mind once him giving you a apple—such a rosy-cheeked one as it wur, too, like a painted picter, for all the world."

"It's chilly standing to-night, Jonathan," said the Rector suddenly. "Thanks for telling us about Sir Marmaduke. Good-night!"

Then the two went home in silence, and the grey mist grew denser to Alison's swimming eyes.

We are all so apt to fancy a wound is healed, are we not? until some hand chances to touch it. Then we wince, and we know that the soreness is only buried deep, not cured.

The village parliament held a long debate

upon the departure of Sir Marmaduke Peyton
for foreign parts. They had felt quite like
the House of Commons, if not the House of
Lords, for some time back, having had such
truly overwhelming and marvellous topics to
open out and disembowel; but the nights
being now cold, preferred to take the cosy
parlour of the Golden Crown as their debat-
ing-place rather than the celebrated "oak
bench." There they gathered in full force
the night after the lord of the manor had
in silent dignity taken his departure no one
knew whither.

They looked at the question this way and
that; they put constructions upon every
aspect of the thing that would have made
Sir Marmaduke's hair stand erect upon his
head "like quills upon the fretful porcupine;"
they told the tripod to "howd his noise"
whenever he opened his mouth, the while
Maister Straw and the portly farmer did the
most of the talking, and Pilkington rapped
the table with the snuffers in a patronising
manner whenever anything was said with

which he thoroughly coincided. This was, however, not often, as he was of a contentious disposition, and considered a certain amount of disputation became his position as apparitor of the church, and, in a way, only second to his reverence the Rector.

They looked at the matter from this standpoint and from that; they induced the rosy-faced landlady to agree now with one side, now with the other; they could not talk over such an important affair with dry throats, so they took the precaution of wetting them systematically with the best liquor the Golden Crown could boast of, and were not, perhaps, as prudent in their libations as on ordinary occasions.

At all events, the farmer betook himself homewards at last in rather a zigzag fashion, and Maister Straw and Pilkington had to prop him up from behind on several occasions; while as for the tripod, he lagged so much that they threatened to leave him altogether.

Conversation was somewhat spasmodic, and

every man (except the tripod, who got no chance) was argumentative.

"It's a rare good thing," said Pilkington, "that Mother Bond's old tumbledown place is razed, as they say, to the ground."

"Who ever heerd talk on a place bein' raised oop, when yo' mean as it be pulled down—eh, Maister 'Paritor?" said the farmer, stopping in the road to have his laugh over a "scholard" like Jimmy Pilkington "comin' a cropper over his wurrds that fashion."

"You're showing your ignorance, my good man," said Pilkington, with an air of withering scorn. "To raze a building is to lay it even with the ground, so as one stone shall not rest upon another, as the book has it."

"To build a house is to pu' it down," roared the farmer. "Pilkington, thee's bin sippin' onct too often outer t' whisky bottle, an' d' not know the top from t' bottom o' nowt. It isn't every man as knows how to measure his liquor wi' wisdom."

They were just about passing the church gates, and a fine silvery moon was shimmering down upon the headstones, and lighting up the long row of pointed windows in the clerestory.

The tripod, with a courage of the kind called Dutch, put his withered old face to the bars, and the rest—your sheep isn't in it with your slightly drunken man for following the first silly lead that presents itself— huddled round him, and listened with grave solemnity to the sonorous bell striking the hour of ten, each note vibrating through the night, and dying away in the distance with a faint thrill and shudder.

Hardly, however, had the last note thus died when a long lugubrious wail came from the very heart of the graveyard, and our topers fell back helter-skelter, the poor tripod left clinging to the gate, while his stick went swirling into the middle of the lane.

"Lord save us! What's yon?" cried the farmer. "Be it a boggart, think yo', same as t'other we know on?"

"Lord knows," said Pilkington, his dignity

"a thing of shreds and tatters," his teeth chattering without will or consent of his own. "I would I wur safe at home, and so do the lot o' you, I warrant. But the thing must be seen into, neighbours; it's i' the churchyard onyway, and happen it's some speerit o' evil."

Again the long, low, heart-broken wail shuddered out through the dark overhanging trees, and even Pilkington's soul fainted within him.

Still, *noblesse oblige*. Was he not fellow-guardian with the Rector of that church, with the appurtenances thereof, and was he not called upon to show a bold front no matter what fearsome thing had to be faced?

"It's one thing for a boggart to set itsel' on a rail in onconsecrated ground, and another to set its foot i' the churchyard. Neighbours, this must be seen into. Follow on to me."

His hand was on the latch; he was un-dismayed even by the repeated cry, weird and uncanny, that at that moment rose and fell.

"Neighbours," he said, and turned him round to rally his followers.

Not a man was in sight save the tripod, who hung on to the gate like a suit of old clothes, making fearful plunges and clutchings in the direction of his stick.

Some distant echo of footsteps, going very quickly too, in the distance, was all the sound that broke the deathly stillness of the frosty night, if we except a sort of squealing remonstrance from the tripod as to the foolhardiness of any mortal man " going up them dratted steps."

Habit was strong upon Pilkington, even in that supreme moment, for he turned upon his whimpering companion and sternly cried—

" Howd thee noise ! "

Which the cunning tripod did, recovering his stick by a sort of crab-like movement, and making off at a pace that would have astonished his friends, if he had any, which may be doubted.

This last desertion was hard on Pilkington, since even such a poor object as the three-legged one—nay, even a dog or a cat—is apt to be a comfort in circumstances like those in which he found himself. Solitude did its work, for the next time the banshee gave out its wailing cry, Pilkington crammed his fingers into his ears, and desisted from shouting derisive epithets at the fast-disappearing figure of the tripod.

Seated on the lowest step of the flight, with his fingers in his ears, Mr. Pilkington "dreed his weird," not, it must be confessed, in a very heroic attitude; but yet with the soul of greatness beating hot within his bosom. A boggart, banshee, or some such "creeter" had got into the churchyard, of which he was the natural guardian. It was not for him to flee with the common herd, and yet his legs seemed to refuse their office when he wanted them to carry him up the steps. Thus halting between two impulses, it came about that Pilkington remained seated on the lowermost step, and, the potent liquor of the Golden

Crown beginning to assert its sway more and
more urgently, sank into a sort of daze, in
which the boggart of Danny Spool with the
watery moonbeams touching its white face
and wide eyes, got mingled up in his dreams
with the thing that cried and wailed among
the graves above him. But it was only in
these turbid visions of his that the banshee
mourned, for silence, broken by the low
whinny of some horse restless in its village
stable, had settled down upon Scarsdale, and
presently Pilkington slept the sleep of the
just.

"Hi! here, Pilkington, what's this? Wake
up, man!" and a hand touched his shoulder.

Pilkington sprang into life like a mechanical
toy of which some one has touched the spring,
and stood stammering and staring before the
Rector, who, wrapped in his big overcoat and
with his flat-crowned garden-hat on his head,
stood by holding a lantern.

Even in that sleepy moment the incon-
gruity of the garden-hat struck Pilkington
unpleasantly.

" 'T'arnt seemly-like as he should go about that way," was his comment on subsequent parliamentary occasions ; " a Rector's a Rector, say what you will, an' I'm none so sure as he ought to ha' carried t' lantern."

Anyway, lantern and all, there stood the Rev. Wentworth Darling, and, most amazing to Pilkington's blinking eyes, behind him Maister Straw and the farmer, while in the near distance that abominable tripod came waggling along on his three legs.

"They've took all the credit of trackin' down this here screech-owl of a boggart to themselves," thought Pilkington, as the crew followed the Rector—looking like a monster glowworm—up the steps.

It will never be known how the tripod mounted that Hill of Difficulty, but there he was, catching his stick in the headstones and stumbling about everywhere, as the party searched the graveyard.

"There is nothing here," said the Rector, peering about ; " you have all been dreaming ; and you, Jonathan, have seriously startled

Mrs. Darling by rushing in in that impetuous manner."

But here he stopped short.

As he stood by Lady Peyton's grave he was conscious of a dark object lying right across it, prone upon the sodden rimy earth.

The men bent down; the lantern was raised high.

"Why, it's t' ould dawg!" cried Jonathan.

The farmer slapped his thigh.

"Danged if it arn't!" said he; "an' hoo's bin bayin' t' mune."

Anyhow, poor Hound would never "bay t' mune" again, for the great paw fell with a soft thud upon the soil as the Rector raised it and let it go.

Looking close at the faithful creature, whose glazed eyes seemed to Pilkington to look like those of the boggart of the mill, they were all struck with the sorry change that had come over him. His bones showed grimly through the tawny skin that hung so loosely over them, and he looked unkempt and neglected. Hound was not an old dog, as we know, but he might have died of old age as he lay there in the flickering light of the lantern with those pitiful faces bending over him. A quavering voice at last broke the silence—

"Our Elizer Anne's cousin on t' mother's side, he's a helper at t' Owd Hall, an' hoo told my missis as t' Squoire used t' pore beast shockin' since my Lady died. T' dawg wur kep' chained oop noight an' day, an' when he moaned sorrowfu' loike, t' Squoire 'ud go out an' lash him wi' 's huntin' crop, that would he."

The men looked fearfully round.

The Rector's hatred of gossip was well known, but the kindly face under the garden-hat, though sad enough, was not angry ; and the tripod, taking fresh heart of grace, and following up the only social success that ever fell to his lot, made bold to say—

"He's broke his 'art, yer reverence, an' died on't."

"His loving, faithful heart," said the Rector.

It will be many long years ere we see

Scarsdale again, and I am sorry to take leave
of these simple people, whom in writing of
I have grown to love; sorry, too, to think of
the changes that must have come about before
we retrace our steps along the mill-bridge and
over the Meadows, before we hear the chiming
of the sweet bell-voices, and catch the ruddy
glare from the window of the Golden Crown.
I know what the march of civilisation means,
and feel that Jollick's—dear, delightful Jollick's
—will be swept away by its oncoming. We
shall listen in vain for the cheery sound of
the guard's horn, and, alas! look in vain for
many a familiar face.

No one could expect the tripod to dodder
on much longer, and it is well, therefore, that
we should take leave of him in his one hour
of triumph, the one and only occasion on
which no one requested him to "howd his
noise."

The sun rises, the river leaps and sparkles,
the fairy tracings of the hoar-frost that outline leaf and gable begin to melt in the warmth
and radiance. Life stirs in the village below

the churchyard, and men are coming up the steps to bear away the body of the dead hound, whose heart has been broken by loneliness. The farmer's overcoat has covered the poor gaunt frame all night, laid there by its owner as a sort of tribute to what his rugged, simple heart recognised as the nobility of a dog's life, the grandeur of a dog's death. And as they bear the faithful creature away, one says that many a Christian is buried in holy ground and deserves it less.

The sun shines lovingly on the little spears of the snowdrops on Lady Peyton's grave, wooing them from their snug retreat. The workers set about their work, the clang of the forge is heard, and the boom of the mill.

Scarsdale wakes up to a new day, and will do to many a day, and many yet to come, which we shall not be there to see.

END OF PART I.

# PART II.

## CHAPTER VIII.

### RIVERSDALE.

LIKE a stream that dives underground and then comes to the surface again, the thread of our story now runs on unseen for a space of close on twenty years. Of course it would have to be a stream in a fairy tale to run for such a space of time underground, and then emerge none the worse for its dip; and, in the same way, the pen claims magic power to do what it will with the creatures of its own creation.

We have left the wilds of Yorkshire, the fir-clad hills, the swelling dales, and billowy wolds, the rugged rocks and quarries, and find ourselves in the heart of the Midlands, surrounded by scenery that is in itself a sort of pastoral symphony—the very harmony and music of Nature when in her gentlest mood.

Riversdale, the small country town in which the interest of our story now centres, lies folded in the arm of a softly flowing river, that runs like a silver streak through rich meadow lands and stretches of tangled underwood.

In summer the green and dimpling grass runs to the water's edge, and the stream is emerald. In autumn the rich corn stands tall and golden, mirroring itself in the ripples, and then the river is palely amber. Great patches of osiers stand close at intervals, and the little coots dart in and out of their welcome shelter, while tiny warblers sway upon the sedges, and the sleek brown head of the water-rat makes a long line of light as he crosses the stream, leaving the ripples sparkling behind him. Here and there, there are pools, deep and dangerous, under the shadow of overhanging trees, and into these, youngsters delight to peep, having been specially warned not to do so.

In some spots the boughs sweep the stream,
gently drifting with the current, and everywhere the slim river-rush trembles and thrills
as the wavelets pass it by.

There is a sudden bend in this fair river,
and there, cradled as it were in its embrace,
nestles the little town of Riversdale—that is,
what is called Old Riversdale.   There are
branches and extensions of quasi-fashionable
streets and villas all round, but the deep-
gabled, oak-beamed, casemented houses are
grouped together round about the grand old
church, with its square tower, whose battle-
ments are clothed upon with a garment of
ivy, and whose lancet-windows are also
framed in greenery.

On a very still clear day you might see
this venerable tower reflected deep down in
the bosom of the river, and even catch the
white gleam of a headstone or two among
gently stirring foliage ; for Riversdale churchyard was a poem and a garden too in summer,
so thickly grew fair blossoms everywhere.
The old porch of the church was alone well

worth a journey to Riversdale, and the broad
stone benches that lined it on either side
made welcome resting-places for frail old
men and women, who somehow managed
to dodder up from the poorer parts of the
town to hearken to what the parson had to
say on Sunday.

Now the Vicar of Riversdale was an important personage in the place. He was a man
of culture and of means, and had in times
past been the loved and longed-for of every
marriageable female in the parish—that is,
among the Church folks. The Nonconfor-
mists "knew themselves better," as one of
the old bedesmen put it, and realised that
they had nothing to do with the game except
to look on and watch the course of events,
which they did with joy and gladness, and the
retailing of many "good" stories and much
sober jesting. But the last move took every
one by surprise, even the closest watchers.

The Vicar went to the Riviera, and returned—married.

A cyclone, a thunderbolt, all the most

violent metaphors in Nature were called into requisition to express the feelings of the inhabitants of Riversdale on this painful occasion.

Some reasonable-minded persons, however, called to mind the fact that the reverend gentleman had never singled out any special lady, maid or widow, by any particular attention; *ergo*, he was perfectly blameless in taking the step just chronicled. Some other astute being remarked that " this was a free country, and a man could marry whom he liked," which remark made a deep and general impression, acting like oil upon troubled waters.

Thus the storm blew over, and though some were still of opinion that it was " not quite nice " of the Vicar to marry " out of the parish," a universal impulse to prepare a warm and hearty greeting for the bride made itself felt.

When she came, the public in general were somewhat chagrined to find they might just as well have left it alone. When we say that she looked at everything through a *pince-nez*, have we not said enough ?

They could not make her see things, those dear Riversdalians, except through that trying medium.

Spinsters of an uncertain age, who swarmed over Riversdale as the locusts upon the land of Egypt, made ready and presented to her an address of welcome. She glanced at it through her *pince-nez*, and it seemed to become as dust and ashes in their sight. They put up a rather lopsided arch over the Vicarage gate, with "Welcome!" picked out in laurel leaves, and as she looked up at it through her *pince-nez*, they thought the leaves might wither, peek, and pine before their very eyes.

Yet she was perfectly well-bred. She was what is called "high-featured," and decidedly highly connected, and had moved amongst what are styled the "best people" all her life. The consequence was she could not understand the shades and distinctions of Riversdale society. The immense gulf that separated a person who "had had" a shop, and one who still occupied that honourable position, was invisible—to her *pince-nez;* she could not realise or comprehend it. The "position" of the local solicitor's wife or the spouse of a consequential railway engineer was an unknown quantity to her; and, to their unspeakable horror, she mixed these ladies up with others whom they "did not know."

"My dear," said the Vicar to her on one occasion, "I fancy that the Highflyers don't quite like meeting the Thornycrofts at your garden-parties."

"Do you really?" said the lady, focussing her lord. "What is the difference between them? It will take me years to learn these people off by heart."

The Rev. Dalrymple Devenish gave it up. It has been said that he was a man of culture; it may even be stated that he was almost a bookworm; also naturally of a somewhat sluggish disposition, and apt to find his truest content and pleasure in the pages of classic lore.

He thought that Anastasia managed the parish capitally, with the assistance of the two curates, who looked up to her as the

most superior of women, and he was well
pleased to live and let live, to turn English
rhymes into elegant Latin verse, reposing,
not exactly under his own fig-tree, but in
the cosy fastnesses of study and garden, only
rousing his dormant energies on the occasion
of some member of his congregation being
seriously ill, or some grave scandal threaten-
ing the parish.   At such time his zeal and
devotion would glow like the iron in the fire
of the forge, and made, perhaps, all the more
impression on the spectators from its rarity.
Still, he thought Anastasia might "sort" her
people better, and that she managed the choir,
the Sunday-school, and mothers' meetings
better than she did her social arrangements.
But Anastasia had lived, metaphorically, on a
high hill; knew a valley when she saw it, but
was unable to "take in" little hollows and
hillocks in the social ground.   Still her tactics
were daring, and, in the end, must meet with
success.   She would learn her lesson in time.
What lesson, indeed, could there be too hard
for her to learn ?

Of course it goes without saying that, like the ring of Saturn round the body of the planet, the county revolved about Riversdale. Yet not in the exclusive way of thirty years back, for the lines of social life, that now in the nineties hang so loosely and get so inextricably mixed, were even then becoming slacker, so that the Highflyers and their congeners by no means despaired of seeing themselves one day disporting on the lawn of the Lord-Lieutenant of the county, or flourishing, together with their offspring, at the hunt-ball held once a year some twenty miles off.

People there were of what is called "good old stock" who had no ambition of this nature, and were very well content where they were and as they were; kindly souls whose hospitable hearts were as bright and sparkling fires, where all might bask in the genial warmth, and find comfort and healing.

The Vicar's wife, naturally, and as to the manner born, mingled with what Mrs. Highflyer called the "tip-top lot;" that is, not those who were occasionally and on supreme occasions in touch with the town, but those who revolved in a small and select coterie, as their ancestors had done before them, smiling and complacent, serenely ignoring alike the struggling parvenu or the contented burgess, and thereby losing much fun, if they had only known it, and also much edification. The Vicar's wife never spoke disparagingly of her husband's parishioners to these magnates; she was too much of a gentlewoman for that; but when she gave a parish tea-party, she asked some of the magnates to come, which they did, to the amazement of all Riversdale, and the utter despair of a clique who had refused the offered hospitality, to show how much superior they were to the bulk of the bidden guests.

"Fancy!" said one of the six daughters of Caleb Thornycroft, a most respectable merchant of the town, "they say Lady Grace Evelyn made tea in the summer parlour, and when she went back to the house she took Dr. Dale's arm! Did you ever hear the like? I suppose there'll be no walking the same side of the road with him this six months to come."

"I don't think Dr. Dale is that kind," said the youngest and quietest of the six girls; "I think he would just as soon help old Dame Owen over the crossing as escort Lady Grace along the Vicar's garden—a great deal sooner, if he thought she really needed help."

Upon this came a burst of raillery more pointed than refined, but the girl neither blushed nor failed to hold her ground.

She was a girl superior to her surroundings, and not without intuitions. She has hit off the character of the young surgeon of Riversdale, Robert Cleveland Dale, for us to a turn, and in a few words; and for that we owe her thanks.

"Robert Dale is a mere nobody, as any one knows," said the mother of the six, with a toss of her be-curled and be-capped head. "His father was nothing but a small farmer——"

"So was our grandfather," put in the

former speaker, looking up once more from her book.

" Suzette, don't be-little your own kith and kin," said her mother sharply.

Just then Robert Dale passed the window of the house, that looked out squarely upon the High Street, as the leading thoroughfare of the town was of course called. One could not see his face clearly, but the square shoulders, well-set head, and swinging walk proclaimed him a man out of the common, whatever his forbears might have been; indeed, it is wonderful what grand results spring sometimes from the tillers of the soil. Maybe the healthy outdoor life, the healthy toil in the fragrant fields, the daily and hourly breathing of the pure fresh air of heaven stand for something, and all at once the breed runs to powerful and healthy brain as well as healthy body, and, like the blossoming of an aloe, something rare and beautiful is given to the world.

We shall have to hear and say a great deal about Robert Dale, surgeon, son of Thomas

Dale, farmer, before we have done, but for the present we will, by your leave, return to some of the salient points of the good town of Riversdale.

It was not an ordinary town by any means; indeed, it may be doubted if, in its own estimation, there was its equal anywhere, making an exception in favour of London, Rome, and one or two other places of like note.

The self-sufficiency of its inhabitants was visible in their general air and demeanour, and it may be said for them that, although split up into factions, and often torn asunder by jealousies and fallings out of the most bitter description, the town would, on occasion, unite to defend a Riversdalian molested from outside.

We have said that Riversdale was not an ordinary town.

Now to give the reasons for this distinction :—

A poet had lived and died there; a battle had been fought and won. Perhaps on the whole the battle was the stronger fact of the two. At all events, it was the most commercially profitable, since jagged daggers, skulls, often with ghastly clefts in them, rusty sword-hilts, and such-like mementoes of the past were ofttimes dug from the soil, and always traded for eagerly with the finders by the committee of the museum.

This museum was the one possession upon which Riversdale set an almost sacred store, and in which all classes, forgetting their bickerings and social tiffs, took a wholesome and pleasant pride.

The museum had to have even a street of its own, and a very pretty and picturesque street it was too, with grey-stone houses, desirably detached, on either side, and only the most refined of shops existed in it, such as a florist's, a fancy-wool shop, and the establishment of a dealer in old oak furniture, that looked as if it had been brought out of the many-gabled, oak-beamed houses in the ancient part of the town and ought to be taken back again.

The museum was a picturesque building, nestling amid greenery of all kinds, with deep old-fashioned window-seats, casemented windows, and a quaint arched door with a rope-bell—that is, a rope with a little round ball of wood at the end, hanging by the jamb.

Behind the house a long garden ran downwards towards the river, ending in a small apple-orchard, whose further limit was washed by the passing current of the stream. Under the apple-trees the ground was all soft green turf, and the marge of the bank in summer-time was one sweet tangle of loosestrife, golden-balls, veronica, and the white stellaria.

At one side of this garden, turned away from the stir and traffic—such as it was—of the street, stood a tiny cottage; rather like the cottage that you see in a stage "set" when the *lever de rideau* is of the pastoral kind, and Phyllis is about to take a heart-rending leave of Corydon at the little wicket gate : yet a cosy nest enough, well provided with coal and wood gratis in winter, and far enough removed from the river-bank to be dry and healthful.

Jasmine peeped in at its dainty casements, ivy crept up its small square, squat chimneys; and in early autumn tall serried rows of bright-hued dahlias and golden-disked sunflowers, made a blaze about its walls.

This was the house of the custodian, the highly-favoured mortal who had unlimited access to the treasures of the museum, and the further privilege of showing the same to the many tourists and visitors who came to Riversdale in the jocund summertide, when the river shone like silver in the sun, and all the country round seemed to be singing in one sweet accord, "With verdure clad."

For the raiment of summer is a fair flowing robe, broidered with marvellous fair flowers and winged birds, cunningly dyed with the blue of the heaven above and the emerald of the earth below, and nowhere did the goddess wear her trailing robes more bravely than in pretty Riversdale.

Gathered together and garnered up in this wonderful museum were many interesting mementoes of " The Battle."

This contest was always spoken of as "the" battle, as though there had been no other battle (to speak of) in the history of our country.

A tattered banner that hung from the high-arched roof of the "great room" in the museum was, there can be no doubt, an object of adoration to many simple souls; and a sword-blade, deeply dented, and bearing a dark stain which it would have been heresy to say was not the nobly shed blood of some long dead Riversdalian, was looked at with eyes of awe and wonder. Some pieces of armour, with an empty casque set atop of them, were not viewed so kindly by juvenile Riversdale. The vizor had an uncanny look, and to see the blaze and gleam of ghostly eyes between the bars would not have astonished some. It was by the whim of a wealthy man now long dead and of a day now past that this museum had been built and endowed, and due provision both of house and living made for a custodian to tend it, watch it, and display it to whomsoever felt their souls fired with a noble curiosity.

From all this it will be seen that the poet of whom mention has been already made was rather thrown in. Truth to tell, his story was a sort of poem in itself, set to a minor key, and not without interest to the people of his native town.

One fact that was never to be forgotten about him was, he was the son of a working carpenter.

There was always great stress laid on the word "working," though, if one comes to think of it, a carpenter who didn't work would have a poor sort of a chance in the battle of life. As Cowper "sang the sofa," so this poet sang "The Battle," and copies of his songs were kept at the museum and sold to visitors for a small sum.

He had been a frail dreamy-eyed boy, in whose teeming brain the swirl and sob of

the river became as living voices speaking
to his fervid soul of deeds of daring in the
past, of the memory of brave men, of the
sorrows of fair women.

People told how this boy-poet would sit by
the riverside and watch the ripples as they
passed, or loiter in the churchyard near the
ancient Bedehouse, where the rooks debated
gravely overhead and the warblers swung on
the rose-garlands among the graves; told
how his own people scoffed at his "odd
ways" and called him bitter names; until
one day a gentleman (I use the word ad-
visedly, since the pith of the matter, to
them, lay in that) came to Riversdale, bringing with him rod and line, and taking up
his abode at the Battle Inn, a picturesque
hostelry near the Old Market Cross. The
coming of this "gentleman" was, then, the
turning-point in the poet's history, for the
saying that a prophet has no honour in his
own country is true until some one comes
from another country and tells everybody
what a fine fellow he is. Then the face of

things changes, and those who scoffed scoff no more. Something is to be made out of the matter; therefore it is not to be despised; nay, rather petted and made much of.

These two—poet and angler—met upon the river-bank, and there, with the forget-me-not dipping its blue eyes in the ripples and the kingcups gleaming in the sun, the dreamy-eyed boy—for he was little more—for the first time in his young life met with a sympathetic mind. He was won to speak of the voices that came to him from river and cloud, from bird and flower; he was led on to show to the stranger's eyes the ill-written rhymes that yet had the divine fire of genius within them; and shortly afterwards Riversdale was startled to learn that a poem by their own poet had appeared in a London paper and "made a stir."

This was news indeed!

The story of their own battle was to be sung by their own poet; they were to be made even more famous than they had been before!

More than one man whose name was not unknown to fame came to visit the young poet of the Midlands. A volume of his work was subscribed for, and at fever-heat the trembling soul waited the moment of the birth of this, his soul—the giving to the world of those precious fancies that had been whispered to him in the rustling woods or by the sobbing stream.

Vain hope! vain yearnings! for before the child of his mind was born the poet lay for ever at rest, with meek hands folded on his breast and dreamy eyes closed.

Perhaps, had the sun of prosperity shone upon his way earlier, the end might have been different; but he had been misunderstood, he had dwelt too much alone, and only after he had passed away did his fame grow and his fellow-townsmen speak of him as "the poet"—a something to be proud of, an added glory to the glory of the battle he had sung.

A little chamber in the museum was devoted to memorials of him, and his portrait—

taken from a poor enough photograph, yet with a look of life about it too—hung over the high carved mantel.

On his grave offerings of flowers were sometimes laid, and at times his lays were recited by aspiring histrions, and doubtless much murdered in the process.

Still, be it never so faulty, fame is fame, and the gifted boy's brother—now an old man, bent with age—made a good thing of it by showing the tiny room in which the poet had once penned his lays.

When our story reaches Riversdale, the dappled fields along the river were gay with buttercups, and the violets nestled in the grassy nooks, scenting the balmy air. All Nature had awakened from her winter sleep, and a good summer was anticipated; good, that is, in its yield of visitors, its harvest of gain.

The early spring had been a time of upheaval and agitation in Riversdale. And on this wise :—

The custodian of the museum, having

grown too blind to see the objects he was supposed to display and to explain, had taken a gentle hint to retire from office, and the post had been thrown open to competition.

Candidates were plentiful, for the cosy nest of a house, and the means to keep it up, were baits not to be despised; and, among the rest, came an application from two foreign ladies, a mother and her daughter.

Riversdale did not think this anything to wonder at, for it reasoned thus :—

Foreigners are naturally an idle lot; *ergo*, they were sure to try and get hold of a tolerably easy berth, which in winter at all events was almost a sinecure. Also foreigners were an impudent lot, witness the Italian men with hurdy-gurdies who come tramping the country in summer, and would play to you whether you wished them or not; *ergo*, what more natural than that these two outlandish creatures should send in their names to the committee, and apply for the post of joint-custodians at the museum?

All this was well enough, and no one

wondered, but when it became known that
the said foreigners were appointed to the
coveted post, Riversdale lifted its hands and
eyes as one man and one woman. They said
they had "no doubt the committee knew its
own business best," and made this observation
with such an air of withering sarcasm that it
was a wonder each several member of the said
committee did not shake in his shoes.

They were always like that, these Riversdalians; always saying they hoped somebody
or other "knew what he was doing," meaning
all the while that he knew nothing about the
matter.

Then this case had very serious aspects.

The mother, a dark, stout, soft-eyed woman,
with long, filbert-shaped nails, and a complexion like a gipsy, was a Roman Catholic.

She had been seen going to early Mass at
the little chapel out by the hospital. It was
very serious.

Simon Budd, the old bedesman who was
told off to answer the door of the museum
and weed the garden, might be corrupted.

Papists always tried to "convert" everybody about them. But some one remembered that, providentially, old Simon Budd was at times somewhat deaf.

There was certainly an element of safety in that.

The daughter—well, no one had as yet seen much of the daughter, for she had been a bit ailing; but rumour had it that she had seen the errors of her mother's creed, and become a member of the Church of England as by law established.

There was some comfort in that.

The fact of these two ladies (no one ever grudged them or withheld from them that title) being foreigners was, however, not so easily to be got over.

It was, of course, possible for a foreigner to be a respectable person, but the probabilities were against it.

These questions were decided with much shakings of head and many tea-drinkings.

It was of no use saying anything to the Vicar's wife, for she had already loudly expressed her satisfaction at people who were sure to be interesting coming to Riversdale. The Vicar would say whatever she said, and the two curates would follow suit. The whole set of them made quite a party, no matter what was under discussion, and gave no one else a chance.

It was therefore resolved—chiefly by the weight of the spinsters aforenamed—that, as a sort of respectful and silent protest against the state of affairs, a Bible—a proper Protestant Bible—should be subscribed for and presented to Mrs., or, as some said, Madame Delano.

"Such a name to have to write in a plain, straightforward English Bible!" said Miss Arabella Beeswing, a tall, gaunt, lantern-jawed female, who sometimes assumed a small sailor-hat, to the great terror of the neighbourhood; "but then, we must be charitable in these things. People cannot help their names, can they?"

The rest—there were about eighteen of them—murmured a faint acquiescence.

It was then decided that the Bible should be a large one, solidly and plainly bound.

"To show the poor misguided creature that it's for use and not for ornament," said the fair Arabella severely, displaying all the muscles in her neck, as she pulled on a tight pair of brown thread gloves.

It was further decided that the print of the book should be large and plain, in order that Madame Delano might have the less difficulty in deciphering it.

This seemed to insinuate that foreigners were probably idiotic as well as wicked, and the covert insinuation was a relief to some of the assembly.

The book was procured and presented.

Madame Delano touched it with those long, soft, olive-tinted fingers of hers, and said, with a graceful little bend of her shapely head—

"I thank you each and all; you are, I am sure, meaning to be kind."

It was not quite what they had expected, and Miss Arabella thought she detected an impudent flash in the eyes of the "slip of a girl" who stood behind her mother during the bald and dreary ceremony of the presentation.

"A most objectionable-looking young person," said Miss Arabella, drawing the chaste shelter of her brown holland dolman about her bony frame; "I really can't think what the committee can have been about. It was General Gildea who gave the casting-vote, and I *must* say——"

"I don't think it would quite do," put in another timidly, "to say anything against General Gildea. You see, being such an old family, and so much thought of, and so highly respected, and all that. . . Why, I have been told that in his old regiment—the 97th, wasn't it?—he was simply adored."

"Fiddlesticks!" said Miss Arabella.

# CHAPTER IX.

## ESTELLE.

" ESTELLE! ESTELLE!! *Estelle!!!* "

Madama Delano was calling through the casement that looked down towards the river, which gleamed like a narrow strip of mirror in the distance. This window was bordered by the leaves of the virginia creeper, still tenderly green, and soon became the frame for a delicately tinted picture, the face of Estelle herself. Not so beautiful a face as had been once that of her mother; any one could see that with half an eye; the features by no means so regular, the eyes not so black and gleaming, the complexion fairer, the hair some shades lighter, and raised like a halo, by its own elastic curl and luxuriance, above a brow broad and intellectual. A bewildering face altogether;

not so much when Estelle was silent as when she spoke or smiled. Then the very sparkle of the river lurked in the clear hazel of her eyes, and her voice—— Ah me! what a voice of music was hers.

No wonder visitors to the museum, being of the lordlier sex, took such a redoubled interest in the old swords and battered helmets, among which grim relics the girl of the sunny smile seemed like a butterfly flitting here and there, and, poising near this memento or that, gave it, from the very force of contrast, a deeper meaning. Madame was, of course, the chief custodian, and having learnt the story of the battle off by heart, repeated it with now and then a pretty gesture of the hands such as would never have suggested itself to an Englishwoman, and helped on the interest amazingly. Estelle might be looked upon as something in the light of an addendum to all this; but then, such a charming addition !

It was a trial to Miss Beeswing and her following that, in spite of this charm, which

even those who most disapproved, and looked
upon it as a sort of contrabrand goods that a
woman would be much more respectable without, could not ignore, not even the smallest
indiscretion could be laid to the young girl's
charge.

Always excepting that of domestic servants,
I suppose there is no class so prone to putting
an evil construction on anything they do not
understand as a gang of women who, never
having had the slightest temptation to step
aside from the strict path of decorum, imagine
every other woman ready to yield to the least
sound of the voice of the charmer—charm he
never so unwisely.

They visited the museum at all sorts of
hours. Like a troop of ragged old vultures
they hovered about their prey, seeking a hole
to pick—yet finding none.

Once or twice they thought they were at
last "on the spot;" once especially, when, as
they tinkled the pendant bell, they heard the
ripple of young laughter.

"Now we have it," they thought; "now

we shall be able to report to the committee frivolous conduct on the part of the assistant custodian, and General Gildea will bite the dust."

They had no patience with the doddering ways of that wretched old Budd, who appeared to be about a quarter of an hour in letting them in, and even then appeared with a senile grin upon his antiquated countenance that was of itself an impertinence.

A still further report to the committee suggested itself.

"Want of alacrity and civility on the part of Simon Budd, bedesman of the town of Riversdale, and inmate of the ancient bedeshouse in the churchyard, so well known to antiquarians."

That would be at once pointed and intellectual, speaking equally well for the vigilance and reading of the framers thereof.

"Budd," said Miss Arabella, with that withering accent so well known among her many friends, "it appears to me there is more noise than is quite seemly in the museum

this afternoon ; more frivolity than the—ahem !
—committee would approve."

"Yes, indeed, Budd," continued another
virgin charmer wearing a hat of the appal-
ing kind called mushroom, and with a bunch
of innocent flowers tucked into her thin flat
waist; "Miss Beeswing is perfectly correct
in her criticism ; there is too much noise—a
great deal too much."

Simon Budd scratched his head.

Then grin number two lighted up his
wrinkled old face.

"I like your quack, ladies," he said, displaying the one tooth he possessed in an
engaging smile ; "I like your quack. Why,
bless yer 'arts ! that be's the Vicar's lady,
that does, an' some of our folk as has come to
see the new battle-axe as you've heerd on."

By this time they were entering the Great
Room, and there "before their very eyes,"
as Miss Arabella put it subsequently, was
Mrs. Dalrymple Devenish, extended in her
usual lounging sort of manner on a cane
bench placed for the convenience of visitors.

Miss Delano stood beside her, and had evidently just been laughing, for the glint was in her eyes as she turned them on the new arrivals, while two bent and ancient bedesmen—more ancient even than Simon Budd — were standing respectfully by, big slouch hats in hand, and they too had also evidently been joining in some passing merriment. The Vicar's wife looked at the ladies through her *pince-nez*, and they began to feel all at once as though they had sneaked in without paying the invariable threepence, and had no business there at all.

The Vicar's wife was very gracious, the portly form of Madame Delano loomed in the distance, and the new battle-axe was duly displayed; but of laughter there was no more, and the ancient bedesmen looked like a couple of undertakers of " ye olden time," so grave were they.

" Well," said the lady of the mushroom hat, " I suppose the Vicar knows his own business best. But I must say——"

" Oh, hush ! " said a younger inquisitor

hastily, " do not bring *him* into the question ! "

Maria Bunsby had been one of the candidates for the Vicar's hand. A gentle melancholy still possessed her : and she was at all times full of a sentimental awe of him and fear of his displeasure, which greatly amused her family and friends.

In order to take up a dropped thread it may here be noted that the appointment of the two foreign ladies to the custodianship of the Battle Museum had, from a disputed point, at one time expanded into a scandal. Riversdale was indeed a hen much given to hatching such unsavoury eggs, though it is only fair to add that these incubations were pretty well confined to a certain limited " set," though they were often seized upon and worried by others outside, and sometimes, alas ! caused much estrangement and dispeace. The scandal about the two custodians ran on this wise :—

General Gildea (retired) had given the casting-vote in their favour. He had evidently taken a keen (Miss Beeswing and her friend Mrs. Ponsonby-Cobb did not hesitate to say a painful) interest in them. There was a mystery somewhere. As a trained pig hunts for truffles, these ladies set to work to try and nose out that mystery. But the search was a difficult one. General Gildea, enclosed in the fastnesses of his ancestral home fourteen miles away, and often absent hunting, shooting, or fishing at his box in Ireland, was as far removed from them as though he were some bright particular star. He was so appallingly out of reach that it made them dizzy to look up at him. Lady Gildea, gentlest, sweetest of women, was beloved by all who knew her, and little short of worshipped in the tiny village that clustered about Ennismore, their beautiful home.

Surely these people dwelt in fastnesses no hand profane could reach !

But the continuous whisperings of tongues can do a good deal, and the Riversdale gossips were not idle.

Just at this juncture returned from a visit to some distant relatives, one Mrs. Smithers, an *esprit fort* in Riversdale, hungry after scandal at all times, and rather soured to find such savoury morsels had been being handed round and she not there to partake. However, for this enforced abstinence she made ample amends by a most hearty meal off every detail she could possibly glean. Red-faced, eager-eyed, open-mouthed, she went from one to the other, comparing notes, adding a delicate touch here and there to complete this or that picture. A widow, with one lean and gawky son, also possessed of sufficient means, Mrs. Smithers had more time to devote to the perfecting of gossip than her other friends. She went about delightedly and with a bold front, scoffing at the Bunsby's timid pleadings on behalf of the accused.

Of the hints and innuendoes that emanated from this clique of backbiters, the half-veiled, half-covered suggestions that crept about here and there, like slimy noisome reptiles rustling through the underwood of some fair demense, what need to tell? We have all seen this sort of thing done; all felt the hopelessness of stemming the muddy tide.

"We all know," said Mrs. Cobb, with what she meant to be an arch smile, but only looked like a leer on a carnival mask, " that army men are not at all particular. Gay sparks—gay sparks at best."

This with a warning finger upraised, as who should warn the galaxy of fair ones gathered about her to beware of such Lotharios. Miss Beeswing turned away her chaste head.

Really there could be no doubt that Mrs. Cobb was at times a trifle too broad!

"I daresay, too," continued this intrepid woman, "that they—the foreigners—made themselves unpleasant; put pressure upon the General, in fact."

"Madame Delano seems so gentle," began the subdued Maria timorously.

"Seems!" cried Miss Beeswing, now fully

present, recovered from her fit of bashfulness. "Seems, indeed! It is the peculiar attribute of such creatures to——seem."

"But we really know nothing," murmured the other again, "and I am sure the Vicar would be greatly annoyed at scandal of this sort being set going in the town."

"Who's going to set it going?" asked Mrs. Cobb. "Are we not speaking with closed doors?"

At this all the rest looked pitiably guilty, for they knew Mrs. Cobb to be a perfect sieve, and that the closing of doors and of windows, and even the stuffing up of chimneys and keyholes, would in no wise prevent her scattering broadcast any bit of scandal she could possibly get hold of.

"Have you not noticed," whispered Mrs. Cobb in the large ear of Mrs. Smithers, but not so low but what the other two heard plain enough, "a look just about the angle of the brow—I mean in the girl; something in the way the hair grows and curls back? I remember once being quite

close to—ahem!—General Gildea——" Then
seeing incredulous looks pass between her
auditors, she added hurriedly, "It was at
a public meeting."

"Quite so!" murmured the others, and
Mrs. Cobb didn't exactly like the way they
said it.

"I might have had many opportunities
of meeting the Gildeas had I chosen to push
myself forward in society here, but such
a course would have been entirely against
my principles, as well as my inclinations,
though, of course, it was optional to me
—to us, I should say—if we had cared to
do so."

"Quite so!" they said again, but every
eye was lowered, every eyebrow raised.

Mrs. Ponsonby-Cobb had to put up with
a good deal of this kind of thing, her talk
being of the kind called "tall," and her
general conversation inflated.

"I am assured," said Miss Beeswing, uneasy at the delicate turn the conversation
had taken, "that there was an interview

—it may be a painful interview—at all
events, one of the Ennismore servants told
my dressmaker that she saw Lady Gildea
herself come out of the room with the tears
running down her face."

"Oh, dear, oh, dear!" said the Bunsby
moaning; "I am sure the Vicar would be very
angry—very indignant, if anything of all this
came to his ears."

"He would naturally be indignant at
people whose past will not bear looking into
—at, in a word, improper persons getting
a footing in the parish."

"We know nothing—we do not know
anything about it *really;* you *know* we
don't!" cried the sensitive Maria, wringing
her hands; "and I'm sure Madame Delano
does not look like an improper person—
not one bit. She looks as if she had known
trouble—deep and bitter trouble; and she
wears a wedding-ring—she does indeed. I
noticed it particularly, because—because of
what all of you have been saying——"

Mrs. Cobb ran her eyebrows up to the

top of her head, and cast a pitying glance at the speaker.

"Really," she said, "Maria Bunsby, considering you are, as we know, on the wrong side of forty, your innocence—or rather, I should say, your ignorance—is as remarkable as it is deplorable."

What might have been the result of this crushing speech can never now be known, for at that instant a rush was made for the window.

General and Mrs. Gildea in their phaeton, the former tooling along with a light and easy hand his two well-known roans, passed down the street, a small by-street called Cupola Street, abutting on the street called Museum. Down, mind you, not up. Towards the museum, not away from it.

"It is shameless, abominable, an insult to every respectable woman in Riversdale!" said Mrs. Cobb, lurking like an ogre in the shade of the curtain.

"Abominable!" echoed Mrs. Smithers, protruding her inquisitive nose in between two of the others. "Abominable! it ought to be exposed. Taking his wife there too. All too confiding, I doubt not; put off with some plausible story, and those two foreign women laughing in their sleeves."

"We know nothing—indeed, we know nothing," moaned Maria Bunsby in the background.

But no one took any heed of her.

And gradually, by dint of talking it over and discussing it from this standpoint and from that, they began to think that they did know "something."

To impart this "something," under strictest rules of secresy, to every one they knew was the next step. It was said that Mrs. Ponsonby-Cobb repeated the whole thing to fourteen people in one afternoon, and Mrs. Smithers retailed it at the top of her voice upon the post-office doorstep to three shrinking and unwilling females, who did not in the least wish to listen to it.

These might be exaggerations of how it flew from one to another, like a streak of lurid light, how it gathered detail as a rolling snowball gathers weight; but anyhow, in the end, the name of a gallant soldier and a noble gentleman, and that of an innocent and much-tried woman, were bespattered with mire, a circumstance of which both were profoundly ignorant.

"Is it the museum bell again, mother?" said Estelle, looking through the frame of leaves, a little pout on her dainty under-lip. "I thought surely business was over for to-day, and there is a new book here, that I want to read. See, I have my little paper-cutter all ready. Oh, I would rather go with my good book to the woods, mother, than take any more people through the Battle room—I mean people like those we had to-day."

Estelle leant her elbow on the sill of the low casement, resting her chin upon her crumpled-up hand. She was dressed in the simplest gown imaginable — indeed, small variety of toilette was hers—but it clasped her slender rounded figure like a glove, and fell in those soft and statue-like folds that none but a gracefully formed woman's dress can. It was plain black—an unvarying rule that Estelle scarcely thought strange, since it had been invariable—and a small black lace ruffle about the throat gave a glimpse now and then of a fine gold chain—only a glimpse, and that but seldom ; yet had this gleam not escaped the lynx eyes of Miss Beeswing and Mrs. Ponsonby-Cobb.

"Those sort of people always have a good deal of jewellery," said the latter significantly ; and it is a proof of what a fervid imagination the lady possessed that those very slender links took the form of "a good deal of jewellery."

In summer, a small round cape falling to the waist—black, to match the dress ; in winter, its fellow, only of soft grey fur ; a simple hat, neither befeathered nor be-flowered—such was Estelle, looked upon with supreme contempt as lacking all " smartness " by the shop-girls and milliners of Riversdale,

but, with perverse inconsistency, gibed at
for the neatness and completeness of her
high-arched feet that trod the ground with
such a dainty grace, and the gloves over
which she was evidently "particular;" a
smart hat, jaunty jacket, and holes in every
finger-end being quite compatible with aspira-
tions after the reputation of a "smart dresser"
in the opinion of the critics aforesaid.

Cape and hat had been duly donned, and
Estelle had set off to read at her leisure under
the chequered shade, but here she was, called
back like a straying child, not best pleased
either at the fact.

"It is not the museum," said Madame;
"it is our kind friend the Doctor Dale."

"He has come to see if you are better,
mother—that is good," and one neatly-shod
foot tapped the ground impatiently.

"Yes, but he has also brought a book for
you.  Come in, Estelle."

Birds, flowers, every beautiful aspect of
Nature, all these Estelle loved; but books
most of all—most of all books.

She rose to the bait at once, and, in a moment more, made her appearance in the little sitting-room.

There, by the table that half filled the small bay-window with its dainty garniture of leaves, stood Robert Cleveland Dale, a book in his hand, a look of eager expectancy in his grave, dark eyes.

"My mother is better?" said Estelle, laying her hand fondly on the elder woman's shoulder. "Ah, you smile. I am glad of that. One could not smile, could one, if she were not better?"

"She is better, much better," said the young surgeon, in his pleasant, hearty voice. And what a pleasant voice it was! To the sick and suffering a voice that cheered like wine; to the sorrowing and sad a voice that could be very low and tender, bringing comfort and courage with its kindly words.

"I am glad," said Estelle.

She spoke English perfectly, but there was now and then an expression, a turn of words, that told she did not come of English stock, and that all her life had not been passed in this sea-girt isle of ours, where our speech, like our manners, is, take us as a nation, apt to be somewhat rugged.

"I have brought you a book, Miss Delano," said Dr. Dale; "a book about birds. You know you told me how many you see flitting about the river whose names you do not know. I have looked out the one you described to me, and I feel sure it is the meadow pipit. See," he ruffled the leaves of the book, "here is a description of the breast —white and gleaming, spotted with dark brown; and here is a picture of the little fellow."

"Ah yes," said Estelle, bringing her hands together with a brisk triumphal movement, "that is he, the rogue. He came fluttering almost to my feet. I thought he was wounded. I put out my hand, perhaps to catch him, and then, piff-paff, away he flew and was gone!"

Dr. Dale was bending over the book, the level golden light touching his dark, crisp locks, cropped closely like a soldier's, and the long capable hand, so strong and helpful in time of need, tender and light as a woman's when handling the wounded limb or touching the fevered brow.

Everything about Robert Dale, even the crisp wave of his hair, seemed to play up to the keynote of the man's character : resolution, determination, a fixed aim and end in life—a love of work, hard work—plenty of it; the more difficult, the more absorbing, the better.

No man is any real good as a surgeon unless he loves the battle, unless he girds up his loins and braces every muscle in the struggle against pain and death. He must love the work; he must love the fight, the contest, the endurance, the pain, the glory of it. Each prolonged life must feel like a medal placed upon his breast; each bitter pang soothed as a laurel-wreath won in desperate encounter with a cruel enemy. It was thus that Robert Dale looked upon life and its duties.

Just now he was taking his ease, a rare

thing for him. He was basking in the sunshine, listening to a strain of sweet and tender music that had only of late stolen in upon his life.

It was a melody the like of which he had not fancied the world contained. Its echo was ever with him, making his work seem lighter, his energies more untiring.

In truth he was in sad case enough, was Robert Cleveland Dale.

He did not, however, look so, as he raised his handsome head from the book, his radiant eyes seeking Estelle's, and taking in every smallest detail of her personality, even the broken gleam of the thin gold chain about her throat.

" See," he said, " here is the description of what your little bird-friend was at—'This is one of the birds which feign being wounded in order to entice intruders away from its nest.'"

"Oh, the sly thing!" said Estelle. " I shall not be sorry for him the next time; I shall know he is only making a make-believe. I shall laugh to his face."

Her eyes looked covetous, as she half shyly peeped at the volume under the doctor's hand; the volume where each bird was limned in all its graciousness of form and colour— here a yellow-hammer, golden as butter made in buttercup-time; there a martin, with his slate-blue wings and gleaming breast.

"Would you like to keep the book awhile?" said the doctor. "I should be so glad to lend it to you."

"You are very good to my daughter," put in Madame Delano, "and she is grateful to you. She will be very careful with that pretty book."

"I shall only value the book the more for——" began the doctor impetuously; then he stopped suddenly, flushed, and "made himself a countenance," as our French neighbours say, by looking out of the window.

In the fading amber light the swallows flitted, rose and fell about the wide eaves of the Museum, floating every now and then as far as the custodian's house, alighting softly on the comb of the roof, or by the upper gables, and then floating back again, like swimmers in a summer sea.

"I think we may call that 'birds at play,'" said Robert Dale.

"Yes, they are sweet," said the girl; "and in the morning when I first wake I love to hear them talk so fast, so fast. They seem to cheer me up and say, 'Keep up your heart, Estelle; one long, long day can only hold one long day's work.'"

Far away, Robert Dale knew not where, gazed the golden-brown eyes; the girl's whole face changed. It was like a landscape over which a shadow has suddenly stolen. No one could have supposed that bright young face had so much latent sadness in it.

The doctor drew a long, deep breath. This fairy music of his had turned to the minor key, and the change bewildered him.

"Do you really—you who are so young and bright—stand in need of being cheered?"

His manner was so respectful, so reverent even, that no *soupçon* of presumption lurked beneath his words.

"Yes," said Estelle, with a weary gesture of her arms. "I am so tired, so tired, sometimes."

Madame Delano frowned, and in a moment the cloud passed, and the girl was on her knees beside her mother, clasping and kissing her, murmuring between the kisses—

"I am never tired of you, never tired of you, mammam *mia!*"

It would be difficult to describe Robert Dale's sensations during this scene.

It was all so new to him, so un-English, so unlike anything that had ever been in his life before—his life of hard grind, hard struggle, hard endeavour. His surroundings had been of the most commonplace in his boyhood—nay, even sordid. The only poetry he had known was the pathos of struggle and resolve, the clarion-note of self-control and high endeavour.

But now this was a picture that dazzled his eyes.

It almost seemed as if both the women had entirely forgotten his presence. But at last

Madame Delano recovered herself. She wiped away a tear that had stolen down her olive cheek. She put Estelle away from her with soft compelling hand.

"There, there," she said, "do not care, *carina;* it is over. I shall no more vex myself. You are ne-vare tired of me, of your poor old mammam, well I know it. . . ."

But as Robert Dale walked home through the falling dusk he asked himself over and over again—

"Of what is she tired, then? and why should she need the swallow's song to cheer her? Ah, . . . dear heart!"

Which shows that Robert Dale was indeed in a bad way.

# CHAPTER X.

A LIFE of resolute effort is, almost of necessity, a noble life.

It cannot, either, be denied that of difficulty is born endeavour, and with this bitter yet wholesome herb the boyhood of Robert Dale had been thickly set. Yet he had faced it as the brave soldier faces the foe. Born among surroundings against which his temperament and ambition girded, when a lesser nature would have grown lax and discontented, he stood firm upon his feet to wrestle manfully with destiny, resolved to make a new world for himself when time should be ripe.

His father, Thomas Dale, farmer, was the worthiest of men, and a most diligent tiller of the ground. His soul was bound up and centred in the task of garnering in from earth's

teeming bosom all she had to give. He could
not be brought to understand why this boy,
the fruit of his loins, in many ways the express image of his person, should yet be cast
in so widely different a mould. Why should
Robert "upset himself" about book-learning
when the crop of wurzels was good, and
the little apple orchard produced as much
rosy-cheeked fruit as though it were a
big apple orchard? The thing wasn't in
reason.

And yet, were not his eyes assailed on all
occasions with strange and unwelcome sights
—sights that caused him to stand "stuck-like"
among the clover, cap in hand, scratching his
head, and feeling quite sorry for the speckled
hen whom he had put to sit on the ducks'
eggs?

"Her'll be zame as me; I'll be zame as
her," said he to his sonsie wife; "feer't o'
what's born to us, both on us."

But the wife looked more kindly upon the
boy's eccentricities.

"Thee knows some o' my forbears were

gentlefolk," she said (not without a smirk);
"happen it's coming out, Thomas man."

"I dunno about that," said the farmer.
"I've a mind to think as we were a bit fullish
in giving the lad a name above himself, as it
were; but you would ha'e yer way, Leezabeth; you would ha'e yer way, zame as
t'other women i' the world."

"Well," said "Leezabeth," flaunting her cap-
strings, "mother's father, John Cleveland, wur
as nigh a gentleman as might he, and I'm
proud on him, and want to have him kep'
i' the family. 'Tisna that as has set up our
Robert wi' notions."

"I dunno," replied the farmer; "I'm none
zo zure. A name ofttimes does a lot o' mischief. See now, there was the dun coo.
Robert would have her ca'ed Daphne, a
young woman of no account, from all he
tells me on her; and hasna that coo bin the
mischief to manage? Why, she'd kick the
pail over soon as look at yer, an' whisk her
tail i' Suzie's eyes first, to blind her! Ah!
but she's an artful one, is that Daphne, zame

as her namesake; for Robert says when a
young man got on too forward to her, she
changed hersel' into a tree; there's wilfulness
for you! Not but what it was to her credit,
as yo' may say; but la! la! what tales be
these to tell to a respectable man! 'Father,'
says that there boy, 'there's no fear the dun
coo'ull turn hersel' into a tree.' 'Maybe,'
says I; 'I'm not so zure o' that. I put no
bounds to her artfulness,' says I,' and at that
t' lad's face wur one great larf. Eh, bo' there's
a deal in a name, Leezabeth—a deal in a
name."

It must not be supposed that the boy
Robert was lazy on the farm. On the contrary, when he could get time from attending
to his schooling, none was handier with the
pitchfork; and as to his furrowing of potatoes,
the lines were as straight and regular as the
sandmarks on the sand left by the retreating
tide. This kind of work he usually did on
half-holidays, for, alack! the grammar-school
of the nearest Somersetshire town was seven
miles away, and what with coming and going

and work-hours, he hadn't much margin left to his days. Seven miles in and seven miles out. How did he come and go ?

On his sturdy legs, to be sure, hail, rain, or shine, starting in the cold, dark winter mornings, and thinking what a lucky boy he was to have a dear, good mother who thought nothing of getting up—not at cockcrow, but long before the old rooster was even awake—to get her son a cup of steaming coffee and a hunch of bread-and-dripping. Then there was the satchel to be packed with bread-and-cheese for dinner.

A hard way of getting schooling, this! Yes; but then this boy loved knowledge as other boys love apples and dough-nuts, and he was so far highly blessed (for in those days education was not what it is now, fruit that any hand may pluck from the tree) in finding a quiet, simple, but most earnest-souled scholar in the head-master of the country school, and to Robert the ancient walls and meagrely furnished rooms of the old foundation became as a grand cathedral of learning, with the old bookworm by way of high priest.

No sooner did this pedagogue find out that a thirsty soul was seeking for water at the springs of knowledge, than, snorting, as it were, like an ancient war-horse at the sound of the battle-call, he took the boy under his special care, and set ordinary hours and rules at defiance.

The young student was asked to dinner at the pedagogue's house, and presented to the pedagogue's wife and daughters. This was a great social rise for "boy Robert," but he took it in the same spirit of simplicity as he did everything else, even stayed over a Sunday in that abode of learning without becoming what the farmer called "heady," a development that worthy man had much feared.

It cannot be denied, however, that after this event "Leezabeth" carried her Sabbath bonnet with a queenlier air, so that neighbours looked and whispered in the churchyard during after-service gatherings and pleasant chats on tombstones, for many in that simple country came from afar, and "hung about" in between morning and evening service. Indeed, one or two old women went so far as to drop a courtesy as Mrs. Dale passed, and say "Good-day to you, marm; and it's fine tellin' as Master Robert be turnin' out such a scholard, and hob-nobbin' wi' the best."

At which Farmer Thomas wrinkled up his nose, making believe to treat the whole thing with unspeakable contempt; but when sitting snug by the house-place fire his wife heard him mutter to himself—

"'*Master* Robert'—oh, indeed! '*Master* Robert,' forsooth! Very good; it's no bad the lad should be respectit an' thought of for his larnin', zure enough."

Then he caught "Leezabeth's" eye upon him, and hummed a stave of "Drumclog" to give himself a countenance—

> "Oh, what is man, that Thou should be
> So mindful of his ways?"

but the good wife knew that her husband's heart was big within him with pride in "boy Robert."

After this it was no shock to the farmer to come across his lad hunched up under a hay-stack with a book upon his knees, or to see him perched aloft in the fork of a tree with a tome cuddled up in his arms.

Fortune favoured the farmer, or rather, perhaps, success rewarded honest labour and true thrift.

The little farm became a large farm, and there came a day when " Leezabeth " went to church in a black silk dress, with a tall son beside her—a son who had passed through some wonderful ordeal, and won a scholarship. " Leezabeth " was bursting with pride, but the softening tears soon came as she knelt in thankfulness beside her boy, aided not a little, no doubt, by the thought that now he would have to leave her, and go to live in some big town full of all snares and godless pastimes invented by the enemy of mankind for the downfall and overthrow of souls.

There were some bright days, however, before this supreme parting came, especially that one when the pedagogue and his wife drove out from the neighbouring town in their own gig (the honour would have been less had it been only a hired vehicle), and took tea at Orchard Farm, now widely extended, and extending on every side.

That tea was a triumph indeed; not the the least part of it the way in which the kind master said, as he hauled himself up into "his own gig"—

"Your son is a credit to you, Mrs. Dale— a credit to you;" and then went on muttering in his absent fashion as he drove along, "a credit to you, Mrs. Dale—a credit to you."

Robert Dale soon made choice of a profession.

He looked around him, and saw disease and suffering and death rife on every hand.

What grander task than to fight such doughty foes?

It is pleasant to know that Thomas Dale and "Leezabeth" lived to see their son attain to an honourable position in his profession; and then, full of years—for they had not married in early life—fell asleep, well pleased with the blessings Heaven had bestowed upon them during their earthly pilgrimage.

Orchard Farm was sold, and with part of the proceeds Robert Dale bought a practice in the Midlands, settled down in Riversdale, there organised a hospital, made himself a reputation, and gradually came to be consulted by the families round, but chiefly loved by the poor for his care and tenderness to them, his noble service to them of what no fee can buy—true sympathy and feeling.

There were, however, a certain number of people in Riversdale who did not think as much of Dr. Dale as they might have done.

He was the son of a "small farmer;" they therefore pleased themselves by imagining they detected signs of a lack of breeding in him. How did they know he was the son of a Somersetshire farmer? How do people invariably get to know these things?

Because, sooner or later—it is really only a question of time—some one turns up who knows all about it, and forthwith a score of tongues, like so many brazen trumpets, blazon the thing everywhere.

"What difference does it make?" cried Susette, the youngest of six, when first Mrs. Smithers and that lot got hold of this piece of news and worried it.

"My dear, don't show your ignorance," said that lady in a withering manner; "it makes all the difference."

When Mrs. Vicar first came to Riversdale people saw that she was taken by the young doctor's manly sense and intellectual gifts.

"Some one ought to warn her," said Mrs. Ponsonby-Cobb, and this ungracious office fell to the lot of Miss Arabella.

If it is possible to imagine that adventurous female feeling shy, it might be said she did so on this occasion. It was the eyeglass—that dreadful double-barrelled kind of eyeglass, with a long tortoise-shell handle—that she feared.

"Don't tell me," said Arabella on one occasion to the shrinking Bunsby; "she can

see as well as you or I can. I can stand
nature, but when people take to adventitious
aids——"

"Oh," cried poor Miss Bunsby, wringing
her hands in pitiable dismay, "do not speak
so of *his* wife!"

"I would say the same of the Archbishop
of Canterbury's wife," said the other, un-
abashed, "if she used such an eyeglass as
that."

Still, once *en route* to inform Mrs. Dalrymple
Devenish of the real social standing of Dr.
Robert Dale, Miss Beeswing was not uncon-
scious of a certain fluttering of the heart.

Mrs. Devenish was at home. The Vicar
was also at home—very much at home—and
the fattest and most genial of the curates was
drinking tea out of a handleless cup, and
talking in an undertone to Mrs. Vicar, apparently quite as much at home as either of
the other two.

When you go anywhere to make yourself
disagreeable, it is always annoying to find
a congregation instead of a unit. One is so

much easier to put to the rout than many, especially if they be at all *liés* together. Now, this particular curate hated Miss Beeswing with a virulent hatred, and always— so far as the laws of politeness could possibly admit—ignored the fact of her presence. The other curate, on the contrary, hating the lady equally, invariably conducted himself as though a wasp had come into the room.

The Vicar was also on the present occasion bored by Miss Beeswing's appearance. Something had gone wrong with the flue of his study chimney, and workmen were there; hence was he—entrenched, as it were, behind a fortress of tables and chairs—absorbed in a classical author with copious notes.

After the usual amenities had passed, Miss Arabella gave a little tremulous cough, and the stout curate looked up sharply.

He knew that cough as the invariable *avant courier* of something unpleasant. At parish meetings how the sound of it used to run down his spine! He always knew that Miss Arabella was about to "ask a question," and that not a pleasant one !·

"It must be very difficult for a stranger coming into a community like ours," began Miss Beeswing, suavely addressing the Vicar's wife, "to—to——"

"To what?" said Mrs. Devenish, and up came the dreadful double eyeglass.

Miss Arabella felt as though she were a lamb being gazed at by a haughty and overbearing vulture; but she was, for all that, resolved to carry out her designs.

"Well, to sort people, you know—to take in who is who, and all that sort of thing."

"To a woman of the world and of society, nothing ought to be difficult," said Mrs. Devenish, speaking, as it were, through the eyeglass.

The curate began to enjoy himself, and poured himself out another cup of tea. He had been a tolerable hand with the gloves in his undergraduate days, and was not without his pugilistic instincts now.

He scented battle in the air, and made merry in his jovial heart.

" Still," persisted Miss Beeswing, rushing on her fate, with a courage worthy of a better cause, " I think a hint or two——"

" Do you mean that you have come here to give me a hint or two on social matters, Miss Beeswing ? "

The curate would have liked to rub his hands together and make a hissing noise between his teeth.

What an afternoon he was having, to be sure !

That " you " and " me " were delicious, a gulf indicated by an intonation.

" I certainly heard that you—that Lady Grace Evelyn—that, in fact, Dr. Dale seemed rather a favourite, . . . rather intimate. . . ."

" Oh, it is about Dr. Dale, is it ?  Now you are interesting."

Mrs. Devenish moved forward on the sofa. She had a paralysing way of looking absent and *distrait* when people said things that did not please her, but there was nothing of that kind visible now. She was one of those women who sparkle when they are pleased and interested. If no one quite understands what I mean by this, I cannot explain it. It is a quality intangible, and that cannot be dissected; but some women possess it, and it is pleasant, and hath a charm.

The curate felt as if a sun-ray had touched him; and the Vicar—the Vicar was always conscious of his wife's moods—looked up with an absent smile from the book that he had, with the profusest apologies, carried away to a distant embrasure.

"I thought that perhaps you were not aware of Robert Dale's history; he *has* a history."

"Delightful!" said Mrs. Devenish; then, turning to the curate—"Mr. Jenkins, is not this delightful?"

Mr. Jenkins, who was in strong inward ecstasies, murmured that "indeed it was," and took a piece of plumcake.

"Robert Dale is a man who has made his

own way; his father was a farmer—a farmer in *quite* a small way. I don't wish to seem to interfere, but it struck me you might like to know."

"And so I do like to know."

But now a change had come over the Vicar's wife; she did not sparkle any more, and she was looking gravely—nay, solemnly—at Miss Arabella through the double *pince-nez*.

"How good and noble he must be to have made his way so well! I do not wonder that his friends are proud of him."

Then she called to her Vicar in his far-off embrasure."

"Dalrymple, Dalrymple, we must ask Dr. Dale to dinner to-morrow. We are disengaged to-morrow, are we not, dear? Yes, to-morrow night. I have been hearing such interesting things about him; it is really quite delightful, like a story-book, you know."

"Yes, he is a very interesting person," said the Vicar, coming to the surface from long diving in classical waters. "Did I not mention to you—— "

"As if you ever mention anything to me!" said Mrs. Devenish, with an ineffable toss of her aristocratic head; "as if you ever mention anything to me until it is dragged from you! I am indebted to Miss Beeswing for this most interesting information concerning our friend the doctor."

Mr. Jenkins could not very well snap his fingers in mid-air, but he longed to do so; nor yet could he cry "Hear, hear," as if he were at a public meeting; but the words kept rising up in his throat like bubbles from a spring, and he felt that he had better go.

He recovered his equanimity out in the open air, and gloated over the remembrance of Miss Arabella's puzzled face, as the Vicar's wife said to him by way of a parting word—

"It will not be long before we have Mrs. Sylvester in our midst now. I have been to look at the house to-day."

As for Miss Arabella herself, she walked home in a most unenviable frame of mind, and then, like the wounded doe, sought comfort in the bosom of Mrs. Ponsonby-Cobb.

"Amelia," she said, "oh, Amelia! I am quite bully-versey; I shall be days in getting over this."

Then she told her story, and the two went on to tea to Mrs. Smithers's, so that the three might worry the thing together.

"I shall not call at the Vicarage for at least six weeks," said Amelia. "It is abominable that you should be treated in such a way, and before that Jenkins, too! Ponsonby would be most indignant if I were put upon in such a manner."

Now, Ponsonby was the meekest creature, which must account for Miss Beeswing and Mrs. Smithers exchanging a furtive smile behind his good lady's broad back.

As for "that Jenkins," he was having a muffin-worry at his lodgings over the pastry-cook's together with his colleague, one Wilkinson, and the two clerics were so noisy that the landlady, in great concern, expressed a hope that they were "not going to take to bad ways, for surely two nicer gentlemen never stepped in shoe-leather."

As the good woman carried in a second relay of smoking hot muffins, she certainly heard Mr. Jenkins say in a suffocated kind of voice—"If you had only seen her." And then—there could be no mistake about it— he made use of the following remarkable expression—"Oh, my wig!"

"Strange words indeed for a minister to utter," said the landlady.

But her better-half took it more calmly.

"There's a deal of words as he might have said," said he, "as is a deal wuss, and means a deal wuss, Marier."

It is a wonderful thing to try and realise how a very insignificant circumstance will sometimes change, or make, or mar the current of a life. Miss Arabella's bit of spite about the doctor of Riversdale did not appear to be more than a very small ripple on the social surface, and yet, as we shall see, like a small stone flung into a pond, its ripples extended, and it had a wide and important bearing on the course of things.

It may be said that Robert Dale himself was astonished, in a quiet, amused sort of way, at the manner in which Mrs. Devenish suddenly singled him out by her kindness and consideration. He thought it odd, too, that one afternoon he had only just sped the parting guest in the form of the "Reverend Jenkins," as his housekeeper called the senior curate, when the "Reverend Wilkinson" was announced; more so still in that each of these worthy men came on the same errand—namely, to ask him to take supper with them at an early date.

"I am growing vastly popular, it seems," he said, laughing at his own reflection in the glass for lack of any better companion; "and I must live up to the situation, that's clear. I expect it's Pilberry's child that has done the trick, poor little beggar! Wasn't it a treat to hear him laugh and crow to-day, and see the tears of joy in the mother's eyes! Those are the grand and shining moments in a doctor's life—the moments in which he realises that he has fought and—won."

Now, Pilberry's child had only escaped death by what is called "the skin of his teeth," though in this case I doubt if the quotation be a very apt one, since it is open to question if Pilberry's child had any teeth at all, or even at most one or two. Be that, however, as it may, he had had a bad time of it, choking till he was black in the face with that awful thing diphtheria, throwing up his little arms and clenching his little fists in the throes of his agony, at sight of which state of things Pilberry himself rushed out into the backyard raving like a madman, and Mrs. Pilberry set up that dreadful shrill whimper that some women will utter at such moments, and that is to me one of the most horrible sounds in nature. But the child was gently and firmly lifted from the mother's knee, and laid across the level part of the bed. The Doctor and his assistant leaned closely over the little struggling form; there was a dreadful gurgling cry, and Mrs. Pilberry put her fingers in her ears and shut her eyes. When she opened them again her baby was calmly breathing on the pillow, and then somebody was sent to fetch Pilberry in from the backyard.

For the moment the little life was saved, but only one step of a heavy uphill road had been taken, and the Doctor never went home that night. Next day came the Vicar, as much "on the spot" as though no such thing as a classical author existed, and as fearless of contagion as it is given to a priest to be, than which I can say no stronger word.

Pilberry was a greengrocer in rather a small way, so sickness was a pull, and rather a violent one, upon his resources; and when the Vicar said, "Send to Mrs. Devenish for anything you want," he was fain to retire once more into the backyard, lest, as he expressed it, "his feelin's should get the better of him."

Step by step was baby led through the difficult path of convalescence, and the fame of the doctor of Riversdale spread far and wide among the poor of the surrounding villages. Hence it came about that, knowing nothing of Miss Beeswing's visit to the Vicar's wife, Robert Dale set down all the kindliness that greeted him on every side to the case of Pilberry the younger, a case in which, as he told everybody till he was tired, he had done no more than any other surgeon would have done, only he had had luck with the matter, for Pilberry and his wife were quiet, temperate, well-living folk, and so their children were healthy-blooded, and ready to mend if they got the chance.

Suzette, the youngest of six, wept for joy when she heard of this young life spared, no doubt one day to be an ornament to the greengrocery business, and lead the donkey, of which Pilberry *père* was the proud possessor. She wept in secret, and her heart was full of joy and pride for the sake of Robert Dale. You see, this small town in the Midlands had its pathetic idylls and its sad heart-histories, just as if it was London, or any place of that sort, though the fields did look so green and innocent, and the birds

sang in such an artless manner! Indeed, that
of Suzette was quite a little poem set in a
minor key, and known only to her own heart.
All this about Pilberry's baby and other
things happened before that great event, the
selection of two foreign ladies to the dual
custodianship of the Museum; consequently
the Robert Dale then treated of was quite a
different person to the Robert Dale of, so to
speak, to-day.

He would indeed have been indignant even
to think of himself as the same man. Sometimes, as some memory came over him, he
would say—" That was before I knew Estelle.
How strange!"

What a silent world it must have been, he
used to think, before the music of her voice
thrilled it through and through, and made it
all tremulous with melody—for him!

He had not lived in Riversdale without knowing that scandal grew luxuriantly
in its verdant dales and lovely sweeping
uplands. He had not yet to learn that it
becomes a man to be desperately jealous over

the good name and fame of the woman he
loves; nor yet that to have his name coupled
with that of Estelle at this present stage
of affairs would do the girl harm, and himself
no good.

So he went about matters artfully and with
subtlety.

Every moment during which he could
watch her supple, graceful movements, watch
the changes of her changeful face, listen to
her gentle prattle, were very precious in his
sight, yet he had to be niggardly in his
grasping of them. He might have said with
the sweet blind poet—

"'Twas dawn when first you came ;"

for indeed to him the advent of the stranger
maiden had been as the dawn of a new
day.

Robert Dale always hoped he was not glad
that Madame Delano was not always well.
He shrank from the idea of finding pleasure
in another's ill fortune ; but still, it was with
a mighty alacrity he was wont to obey the

summons, sent by Budd, to go and visit Madame Delano.

Listen to Simon's own account of the position of matters on one occasion :—

"I'd scarce oppened my mouth to ax if he were within, when the Doctor he nigh jumped a-top o' me, an', says he, 'Is it Simon?' 'Simon it be's,' say I. 'Tell 'em I'll be there in a jiffy,' says he, an' his eyes were like the stars of a frosty night. 'There be's no kind of hurry,' says I, soothin'-like, 'for Madam's not that bad, only a bit poorly-like an' squirmy, as you may say.'"

This was his tale to Miss Delano—or "little miss," as the old man was impudent enough to call her to his fellow-bedesmen of a Sunday, when they all walked to church in style, clad in dazzlingly white smocks, cunningly gathered and embroided at the shoulders, and slouch-hats shading their dear, lined old faces.

"How kind is our good Doctor!" said Estelle. "Ah, mammam *mia*, but we are rich in the friends we have in this place!"

Half an hour later Robert Dale was at the little house by the orchard, doubly assiduous in his care for Madame's ailments in consequence of that lurking guilty notion of some gratitude being called for because of them.

His patient was weak and nervous; beset, too, with fears lest her health should fail, and so the home—the little, quiet home that she had grown to love already—be taken from her.

When all this had been listened to patiently, when a calming draught had been prescribed for the "too quick beating of the heart," Robert Dale went down into the small parlour, to find Estelle there alone.

She told him how she had enjoyed reading the Book of Birds, how she had identified many of her river friends; and her auditor listened entranced.

What a love of Nature the girl had, what keen intuitions, what powers of appreciation! Then she was so tender over every living thing—every creature in whom the Great

Creator had put breath. He thought of the poet Blake's divine lines—

> "A skylark wounded on the wing
> Doth make a cherub cease to sing."

That was Estelle all over.

A butterfly crushed in a child's careless hand, a bird with drooping wing and fast-dimming eye, these were sorrows deep and real to this girl, whose creed was love.

Then what gestures she made with her slim, pretty hands! Why, they had a language of their own, a speech unique and matchless.

Do not suppose that the young Doctor conducted himself outwardly like a lover. Estelle would quickly have shrunk from that.

He was not so simple. He wooed her on to trust him as a friend, to confide in him, to look to him for help and comfort.

The rest would come in its own time, so he said to his own heart; so he murmured as he sat by his solitary fire, the day's work done; so he told his great brown-eyed retriever,

Sam ; and Sam sat up on end, and looked as if he knew all about it, and was very glad indeed, waving his tail grandly, after the manner of dogs when they wish you to understand they are pleased because you are.

But the time was not yet.

Frank and fearless in many ways, Estelle was still Estelle.

A creature so sensitive, you could never be sure how she would take anything; she must be won, not startled into loving—so thought Robert Dale.

When she had done telling him about the Book of Birds, she spoke of her mother.

" I am not afraid," she said ; " it is not much. If it was much I should die of fear. Mammam *mia* is all my world, as I am hers. There is no other world for either of us than each other. It is like that. But now, it is no wonder she is sick—on this our very saddest day of the whole long year."

Robert hated to feel the hot flush stealing to his face. No one could live among the people of Riversdale as he did and be ignorant of the gossip that obtained amongst them. He was ashamed before the girl's innocent, grave eyes.

"You mean," he said, looking steadily away from her, "the day your father died?"

He managed to convey a world of reverence and sympathy into the last words, and Estelle's eyes swam.

"My dear, beautiful father was drowned."

The Doctor drew a long breath.

"Do you, then, remember him?"

"I! Oh, I was not born; he never saw me, never knew me, never loved me. In that mammam is richer than I; but I have seen his face, she has it pictured, and it is the face of an angel. It smiles at me as if it would say, 'I know you are my little Estelle, the little girl God gave me when I was not there to see.' Mammam has had such sorrow; she holds it ever in her memory. He left her, he did not know; he nev-are said 'Good-bye.' His sword was by his side, he wore his brave red coat, when last she saw him—she ever thinks of him like that."

" He was a soldier, then ? "

The Doctor's voice sounded rather hoarse. The flush had died from his cheek, leaving it paler than usual.

" Yes, a soldier; a brave, brave soldier. To-morrow we shall speak of him all day when we are alone, and we shall pray; we shall take out the beautiful picture, and put some flowers close before it. We shall fancy he is alive and with us still."

" Was your father, then, Captain, or perhaps Colonel Delano ? "

" No ; that is my mother's name—her own name. We take it because it is, for now, the best to be so. It must be the best, because mammam says so."

" And your father's name ? "

He spoke almost under his breath. It seemed a shameful thing to question this simple child, and yet something urged him on. When the answer came, he wished that the question had never been put.

"I do not know," said Estelle, looking up at him with wide, grave eyes. "I do not know. To me he is my father, just that; always my dear brave father—who is dead."

# CHAPTER XI.

## " BELLE NUIT."

IT may truly be said that, from the day of that momentous interview with Miss Delano, Robert Dale went about his work in a whirl of disturbed thought and wild, though suppressed, unrest.

We all know what it is to be conscious of thoughts of which we are ashamed—ideas that will rise up like hissing serpent-heads, watching us with narrowed, evil eyes—eyes whose glance we strive to evade in vain. In spite of himself he began to think there might be some truth in what the Riversdale gossips hinted at.

When next Madame Delano needed his services, the Doctor felt it hard to meet the soft, dreamy Southern eyes that always seemed to be looking, looking, looking somewhere very far away.

He recalled Estelle's words.

"She has had great sorrows; she holds their memory in her heart—in her heart. . . ."

And yet he could suspect this woman of —— What?

Of falsifying her own life to make it seem smooth and fair in the eyes of her child. Could it be that that "most sad day of all the year" was a fiction, evolved out of love and sorrow?

What of that beautiful bright-faced man in the "brave red coat"? How was he lost? Did he really die, or had he only died out of a woman's life; and had chance —a strange chance, it might be (but then chances are so strange and wonderful, truth so much more strange and wonderful than fiction)—brought her across his path once more, and given him the opportunity of be-friending her—her and the child Estelle?

As to Lady Gildea, Robert Dale had known cases of such noble self-conquest, such majesty of self-devotion, among women, that he could put no bounds in his own mind to what she might be capable of for the sake of her husband. It is not for nothing that a man is a student at one of our great hospitals. There he is a spectator of some of the grandest—because some of the saddest—of the dramas of human life. Intense sadness always rises to grandeur, and what can be at once so sad and so grand as the way in which women will fight against yielding to disease and death, for the sake of those who are dependent upon their loving ministrations?

Having had eyes to see and a heart to feel, Robert Dale had learnt many a holy lesson in his student days, and therefore now he dare set no limit to a woman's generous large-heartedness.

If Madame Delano had been one of those who, loving not wisely but too well, had never sat down to count the cost of all she gave, then also had she been one whose whole life was consecrated to the memory of an ungrudging love. It is not only women that are wives who can be faithful "even unto death," and

here in Madame Delano he was well assured
was a loving and faithful nature.  Had love
also taught her cunning ?  Had the passionate
love for the father resulted in the passionate
love for the child ?  Had that child's love
and reverence become a necessity—a thing
to be clutched at and grapsed, no matter at
what cost ?  Had General Gildea thrown himself upon the generosity of a noble woman ?
Had this sudden renewal of old associations
been wholly accidental, or had Estelle's mother
tracked down the lover of her youth ?  Robert
Dale's cheek flushed hotly as he thought such
thoughts as these.

His mind, that had been clear as a running
stream, had now grown like a wind-swept
lake, where shadows chase each other, and
the tossing ripples babble under overhanging
boughs.

He tried to tear away his thoughts altogether from the mother and daughter and
their affairs.  He tried to convince himself
that he longed for the old passionless, un-
troubled calm of the past.  But in his heart

he knew that it was only now he *lived*, and that the pain, and the trouble, and the seething thought were but as a darksome, haunted wood in whose heart a bird sang.

Out in the quiet country he rode his grey mare Bess at a breakneck pace, finding a curious satisfaction in the rush and the hurry; the while Sam, fancying, no doubt, that his master was possessed (as, indeed, it may be said he was), tore along, *ventre à terre*, with lolling tongue, and wild eyes raised to the flying figures of the mare and its rider. Sam doubtless also judged his master to be inconsistent; for why, after all this display of energy in the far-away lanes and fields, did Dr. Dale sit staring into the fire, head on hand, taking but little notice of the personage in a curly brown coat who would have been glad to suggest that tea had been on the table some time, and it might be that a little milk in a saucer would be agreeable to a thirsty dog?

But Sam had not read Guy de Maupassant;

he did not realise the truth that *tout semble
mort après ces crises de vie.* The demon of
unrest being allowed its fling, leaves an un-
natural calm behind, and while that lasts
the mind lies fallow, and the body is lapped
in a delicious lassitude.

In fancy Estelle's eyes met Robert Dale's
as he sat dreaming half through the night;
Estelle's voice seemed murmuring in his ear;
and Sam would turn round seven times, fling
himself down with a thud and a sigh, and
resolve to wait, like the patient soul he was,
until his turn should come again.

Things were not made better for Robert
Dale by another interview—this time a chance
one—with Madame Delano's daughter.

Returning from what he called a "sharp
walk," that was, some eight miles across
country to visit a distant patient, and back
again, the Doctor overtook Estelle returning
from a riverside stroll.

Sam was the first to discover the slight
black figure among the green tangle of the
larch wood, and straightway set himself to

such mad barkings and gambols of delight that his master's attention was caught.

Surely the sun shone out brighter as she turned to meet him; the water sparkled with a more dazzling glitter! A bird on the lowermost branch of a larch set up a succession of mad roulades and trills, as if he knew the spirit of rejoicing was abroad. Pacing side by side, these two drifted into talk; Sam scouring along with his nose to the ground as if on some vastly important trail, and then making sudden stops and leaps—behaving, indeed, as the Doctor said, laughing, "like a kid."

"He is always glad to see me like that," said Estelle; "if he meets me all alone he is the very same. I know not why he so much likes to see me."

The rejoinder was evident, but the Doctor refrained himself.

There was another subject, however, upon which he was determined to venture.

"Do you remember, Miss Delano, what you once said to me about the swallows?" he began almost timidly. "I mean about them twittering in the morning, and—and cheering you up, you know. I have often wondered since—pray do not think me impertinent— what it was that——"

"Made me glad to hear those birds so cheerfully singing?" she put in, seeing him hesitate.

"Pray do not think me impertinent," he said, the colour rising slightly in his bronzed cheek.

"Ah no!" said Estelle. "No one is impertinent that is kind, and you are so kind to us always. I am glad to tell you— I am glad to tell anybody. It was that Museum."

"What!" he said, smiling; "the battle?"

"No, no," she answered, with a charming gesture of the hands. "The people who come to see the battle; the battle is itself fine— very, very good. But ah! they are so what you call wearisome; they talk and talk— some do yawn and yawn; and they do not care—they do not care." Here she looked like a bird with ruffled plumage and perked head. "That is the worst of all: they do not care. They come because everybody comes. 'Is that so?' they say; but they do not believe. It is not in their hearts— only in their eyes, their dull-as-stupid eyes. Ah, why did the good God make so many tiresome people in the world—and why do they all come to this place?"

"I never thought of it," said the Doctor gravely; "I never thought how trying it must be for you—all day and every day, week in and week out. And Madame Delano, does she feel it too?"

"But no, oh no; she is so good. To mammam *mia* no-body is e-vare tiresome; she is so much more good than I, she is sweet as sweet. There is no one like her, not one little bit."

"I am sure of that," said her listener gravely.

Estelle gave him a soft, grateful look that set his heart throbbing thick and fast. It may as well be said now that in the eyes of

this young girl the Riversdale doctor appeared
a grave and reverend senior, one that might
be dealt candidly with on all points. His
age doubled itself in her mind's eye, and there
can be no doubt he would have been greatly
startled had he realised the standpoint from
which she looked at him. That he was good,
kind, to be ever and always trusted—to these
questions Estelle would have returned a happy
" Yes ; " but a lover——

Ah me, how the merry peal of her laughter
would have rung out like silver bells !

He was big, strong, clever, good, but there
it ended.

She had no fear in saying anything to him
—none. A child could not have been more
fearless of a parent.

"This must I say," said Estelle, after a
little silence, during which Sam had paced
gravely beside the two, a demure mood having
now seized him; "Mammam would not be
happy to know I have spoken such words and
thought such thoughts ; she wills that for
me all should be sunshine ; she would that I

should sing always like a bird that is glad in its little heart. She wept when I said that I was sometimes sad, and while I wiped the tears from her cheeks I vowed that I should never be sad no more, but the sadness came along with the tiresome people. But I am wrong, I know it; I am what you call un-grate-ful. I am like the daughters of the poor King Lear, about whom your great Shake-speare sings; I am un-grate-ful."

"Nay, I am sure you are not that," said the Doctor; "it is the monotony, the routine, that galls you, and it is natural to the very young to feel like that."

He spoke as though he were speaking to a troubled child, and she the while looked up at him with a child's pure and wistful eyes.

"Ah yes," she said; "you mean one, two, three days, all the same; then three more; and three more to that; but then, we must work to live; and see how poor—how poor we were before we came to Reeversdale, before we came to live by the beautiful shining river."

"Poor?" he said, catching his breath a little at the thought.

She clasped her small brown, gloveless hands together, and her lip quivered.

"Yes, that was in France; sometimes we were hungry, and mammam would say that she was ill and could not eat, that I might have the more. There was once an old priest who was so good to us, but he died. He blest me, with his hands upon my head, and then—he died. How sad we were as we looked upon his gentle face with the flowers all about it, and the holy cross upon his breast!"

"My dear child, my poor child!" said the man by her side, and if Estelle had known more of men she would have recognised the love-thrill in those simple words.

But she gave no heed. It was not strange to her that he should call her "child." Of course she was a child—to him. Still, some warning came over her that she was speaking perhaps too freely; some remembrance came over her of a caution given to her by her mother, a caution of which she had been unmindful. But surely it did not matter much. It was only the Doctor after all whom she had been chattering to.

"There are some pleasant things here," she began, hoping to give a brighter turn to the conversation; "Some people are nice, some are kind. There is General Gildea. Ah, see, you have struck that fair tall flower with your stick and killed it; are you not sorry? It will lie there now, and wither away, while all its fellows stand straight in the sunshine. You made me start and forget my words, you were so sudden. Where was I? Oh, I know; I was telling of General Gildea. He has such a kind sweet voice, such gentle ways; and do you know, I think that some-where, at some time, he must have known some one I am like? He held my hand so long a time; he looked into my face, and I saw the tears—yes, real bright tears—come into his eyes. Indeed it is true; I was not dreaming. Mamma covered her dear face, and then he said, 'So like, so like,' speaking, I am sure, not to me, but to some memory that was far away and dear. I know how they look when they speak of things like that, for I have seen mammam many times and often."

Goodness knows how it was that in listening to this girl's artless prattle Robert Dale seemed to be drawn quite closely to her—how it came about that a bridge was thrown across the chasm of the years, and they two, strangers but a little while ago, became as old friends, sharing one another's thoughts and feelings.

Every artless word she uttered puzzled her listener more and more.

What was this mystery that surrounded these women? How was that grand old soldier, General Gildea, entangled in the web?

Could it be as people said?

A man who has passed through the ordeal of hospital life is not apt to be a prude; he knows life, he knows men.

Nothing was wonderful to him in the matter except that "poverty" of which Estelle had told him, and the inexplicable

idea of General Gildea having a hand in the
mother and daughter settling down almost—
speaking loosely—at his own door.

The "Gildeas," as Mrs. Smithers loved to
call them—thereby thinking that, at all
events to strangers, she gave the notion that
she was on quite friendly terms with them—
were a proverb for married happiness, and
the General's manner to his wife had all that
chivalry and devotion that so seldom survive
the bridal days. Whatever steps had been
taken—of this Robert Dale was very sure—
had been taken in concert the one with the
other. No one could see the pair and imagine
for a moment that the one held reservations
from the other.

Thus far the Doctor could reason. The rest
was mere speculation.

He did not prolong that delightful walk
along the river-bank among the kingcups
and the veronica. He was on the alert all
the time, for might not Mrs. Ponsonby-Cobb
or the immaculate Beeswing be taking a
saunter too?

And then—well, he knew what then pretty well.

A tiny bunch of blue-eyed veronica nestled in the bosom of Estelle's dress, and the Doctor looked at it hungrily. At last, just as he was leaving her to visit an entirely imaginary patient, the craving grew imperative.

"Give me those flowers," he said, with that sort of masterful air that sat so well on him; then he added gently, "will you?" by way of softening the demand.

Estelle looked at him surprised.

"They are beginning to fade," she said; nevertheless her fingers were busy unfastening them, and soon they were in his hand. "You are too lazy to gather flowers for yourself," said Estelle, with a roguish look.

"Perhaps so," he added dryly. "And now good-bye."

With his dark head bared, there he stood before her, manly and handsome, and again Estelle thought to herself—

"He is very good, this English doctor. He is a true friend for us."

Besides all the rest, she had told him something more. During the latter part of their conversation she had said—

"You know I was born in a convent. All my first memories are of that quiet life—the nuns in their dark dresses and white veils, and the sweet chanting in the chapel. Oh yes, I remember all that, and mamma on her knees crying by the altar. When I think of things I can see the great tall window behind the Pix, and the pictures on the glass—the Christ, with such a beautiful sad face. I used to think He looked as if He was sorry for us two—as if He knew——"

"Of course He knew; of course He was sorry," the Doctor had said quickly, not without a flush either, for he was not a man given to talk religion, and the words seemed to come strangely from his lips.

So Estelle was born in a convent. Well, well, the tangle of her life seemed hard enough to unravel; but there is one hand that solves the most complicated puzzle, and one hand alone—time. If you want to know anything you have nothing to do but wait, and see that you wait long enough.

Some day, somewhere, the clue that you have longed for will be put into your hand, perhaps when you are least expecting it.

It may be surmised that, even if Miss Beeswing had met these two friends wandering by the river's brim, she would scarcely have given her usual close attention to the matter, as she was now altogether absorbed, body and mind, in a deeply interesting social event—viz., the arrival of Mrs. Sylvester at Riversdale.

From the date of her unfortunate visit to the Vicarage, of which chronicle has been already made, no word of what she had then gleaned as to the expected advent of some one in whom Mrs. Devenish was interested had reached her. She saw by the wicked glint in Mr. Jenkins's eye, when they chanced to meet, that he was well aware of her raging curiosity; but she knew better than to ask him any questions, as he had a nasty way of what she called "wriggling," and had, on more than one occasion, tried to "throw dust in her eyes."

Questioning "little Wilkinson," as they called the junior curate, was also not to be thought of. He, too, was absolutely untrustworthy, and would go sneaking to the burly Jenkins on the smallest opportunity, the two evolving wicked plans together for the overthrow of the (female) parish in general.

Therefore Miss Beeswing had to wait; since to question, or even throw out a hint to the Vicar's wife, could not be contemplated for a single moment. Fancy what an expression would scintillate through the double *pince-nez!*

At last rumour arose in its might, and Riversdale learnt, with a mixture of curiosity and delight, that an ancient manor called Rosedale, some three miles out of the town, had been taken on a long lease by Mrs. Sylvester; learnt with still greater avidity that the lady in question was the widow of an officer; was in her own right rich, though—Heaven only knows how they got to know this!—she would lose the bulk of her wealth if she married again ; and last, but not least, she was Mrs. Devenish's sister.

"As I hear," said Mrs. Ponsonby-Cobb, smoothing down her puce satin, that had been turned three times and cleaned twice, "her husband was a general in the army."

A general out of the army—the Salvation Army not then having come into existence— being a rather rare kind of bird, this information might be considered somewhat hazy.

"I also hear that she is remarkably handsome, brilliantly accomplished, and will in every way be a valuable addition to Riversdale socially."

"If she's all that, she's not likely to favour us with much of her society," said the unfortunate Miss Bunsby, bringing a perfect storm of disapprobation upon her devoted head by the remark.

"I consider Rosedale quite within calling distance," said Mrs. Cobb, undismayed by the many snubs she had already received from new settlers in the neighbourhood, who had really at various times behaved in a most unkind manner.

"Well," said the Bunsby, so rampant upon this occasion that the rest gazed at her in blank amaze, as one might upon a rabbit sitting up and hitting straight out from the shoulder, "I am not at all sure that it is a wise thing to call upon strangers until you know——"

"Know what?" said Mrs. Cobb, speaking like a snapping turtle.

"That you will be welcome," said the Bunsby. "Don't you remember the Fitz-gibbons, who said they were not at home when you called the second time, and then you saw her at an upper window?"

Mrs. Cobb's cheeks matched the puce dress. She breathed heavily; but the Bunsby would not be silenced.

"And you know, when you told everybody how intimate you were there, and how Mrs. Fitzgibbon couldn't do anything without consulting you, she said straight out plain, 'What a liar that——'"

"Miss Bunsby, Miss Bunsby!" cried Mrs. Smithers, tapping the table sharply, "you are drifting away from the subject in hand. Pray be reasonable."

"Besides speaking of people who are really better forgotten," put in Mrs. Cobb meekly.

Indeed, she was utterly routed, but nevertheless registered a vow that she would take it out of Bunsby yet, one of these days.

Mrs. Sylvester came, Mrs. Sylvester saw— or rather,' was seen — Mrs. Sylvester conquered. She was like the Vicar's wife, only more so. *Pince-nez's* were evidently in the family, so one must make up one's mind to put up with that. She was, however, in various other ways most astonishing, and very few alien topics were touched upon for some weeks after her arrival. A dark, slim woman—("almost foreign-looking," said Mrs. Smithers)—with the air of one who has her world at the tip of her fingers; an oval face, strongly marked brows, a shaded upper lip, and a *svelte* swaying figure that could carry off the most *bizarre* costume with grace and refinement; her hair, black as night, curled over the forehead in little shining rings; and when she laughed she showed an arc of small transparently white teeth.

How old was she?

They could not make up their minds on that head in the least.

Younger than Mrs. Devenish? No, decidedly not; but then Mrs. Smithers had already expressed her conviction that that lady was "no chicken," which, as she never set up for a chicken, didn't seem to matter much.

Mrs. Sylvester wore a costume that startled Riversdale, and that yet seemed as if it "grew upon her," as more than one was obliged to acknowledge. It was a long upper garment of tawny yellow, opening over a petticoat of a paler tint, while round the throat was a high ruff of orange-tawny feathers. A small capote bonnet of the same hue completed this wonderful toilet; and thus comparisoned, the Vicar's wife's sister returned her calls. These were many and divers, and it may be said that Mrs.

Sylvester was made aware of the existence of many persons that were absolutely unique in her experience of life.

That she was conscious of the subtle joy peculiar to the naturalist in the study of "specimens" cannot be denied; but one experience of this study was enough for her. Her yellow skirts, floating across the threshold of Miss Beeswing's chaste abode, trailed there for the first and also for the last time; and the same might be said of various other residences.

To her sister she said—

"Your people are quite too wonderful; but a little of them goes a long way. Anything so fearful as Mrs. What's-her-name Cobb and the other woman I never saw. I really had no idea such people existed. As for Mrs. Smithers, when I was sitting in the library I heard her talking at The Lodge, and that, you know, is nearly a quarter of a mile off."

"You see they are Dalrymple's parishioners," said Mrs. Vicar.

"But they are not mine," replied her sister, and Mrs. Devenish knew that Rosedale would see them no more.

However, it came about that the Vicar determined to give a parish party, and Lady Grace and various other magnates were bidden to meet what Mrs. Sylvester vaguely described as "the rest of the crowd."

Be it understood that there were some really nice and cultured people in Riversdale, but it so chances that our story is not concerned with them. These, too, of course, were bidden to the feast, and to these Mrs. Sylvester made herself charming, as her manner was, and fascinated the men and women alike—also as her manner was.

One or two passages of arms she also indulged in, as for instance, when a young man of most affected and pretentious manners languidly explained to her the social difficulties of "our town."

"It is so hard," he said, propping himself up against a doorway in order to gain a firm footing, as it were—"it is so hard to know who to know, don't you know?"

"I am sure," said Mrs. Sylvester, "if I lived in Riversdale I should have no difficulty in knowing who *not* to know."

He was a very superior sort of young man, was this. He wore his hair long behind and his moustache long in front, and had a frameless eyeglass that he was for ever screwing into his eye. He used to impose upon various small fry who came to Riversdale for the fishing and boating in summer, and they imagined him to be something rather above his surroundings, but, as a matter of fact, he was the son of a highly respectable tradesman, who, having been honest and persevering, made more than a competency, retired from his shop, devoted his well-earned wealth to educating his son, and lived and died honoured and respected. Perhaps it is only in a small country town that such a state of things can exist, for where society is limited the best has to be made of every one, and no material, however coarse its woof and warp, allowed to go to waste. Another peculiarity of Riversdale was that the oftener you went bankrupt the more you appeared to be thought of. You paid two shillings in the pound, went near to ruin a confiding tradesman or two, then trotted merrily on and had another " real good time." Or you kept a shop, retired, and straightway gave yourself airs to those who still earned an honourable living behind that bar sinister— the counter.

On the other hand, the trade-class was beginning to assert itself. By this I mean the tradesmen who wished to be nothing else, and were proud of their own standing, and aped no higher or better one. The dawn of that great educational movement that now floods the whole land like a great wave of light was just then breaking in the social sky. A young men's debating society, a reading-room and library, these things and others akin to them were springing up here and there. The Vicar was deeply interested in such matters, his wife scarcely less so, and

Mrs. Sylvester gave such grand and generous donations in aid of these various movements as stirred the pulses of the town and put new life and energy into every one.

But we are drifting from the Vicar's parish party, and must retrace our steps to the pleasant lawns and woods that surrounded the parsonage-house.

Here there were gathered together all sorts and conditions of men and women ; and any one was allowed, indeed encouraged, to show off, and assist in entertaining the rest, as seemed best in their eyes. Mr. Ellerby Jones —the gentleman who was so fastidious as to his social surroundings—recited a poem (of his own composition) entitled " The Lady Araminta ;" a young artisan from a distant village (discovered by Lady Grace, and by her brought forward at temperance tea-meetings and other dazzling entertainments) sang a (quite proper) comic song in excellent style, and being almost wildly encored, gave " On the Banks of Allan Water" with so much music and pathos, that several stout motherly women melted into tears, and said, "Wasn't it a shame, now, that no one could look after the girl better than to let her go maundering about with a good-for-nothing soldier like that!" which showed that Lady Grace's *protegé* had what is called "taken his audience," and made them feel. After this a glee was given in the long low drawing-room that looked out upon the velvet-green sward, mottled with the shadows of cedar-boughs and studded with massed flowers in tubs.

Now it must be confessed that when it took to amateur music Riversdale was very terrible, in spite of which its concerts were generally successful, since everybody went to hear their own relations sing, and consequently everything was encored by somebody; in fact, the local paper (a single sheet, but much thought of) was wont to declare that on such and such an occasion "a thrill of ecstasy ran through the crowded assembly," a statement that was highly satisfactory to all parties, since each one thought that his or her belongings had caused the said thrill of wild delight. But Mrs. Devenish and her sister were accomplished and passionate musicians, and the thrills they experienced were the reverse of ecstatic.

The glee chosen for the present occasion was "Come where my love lies dreaming," and the noise was tremendous. Little chance indeed would his love, or anybody's love, have of dreaming long!

Mr. Jenkins boomed away in the bass, "Little Wilkinson" piped away in the alto, Susette and two of her sisters were the sopranos (all very much frightened, and holding on to each other), while the contralto parts were taken by two brazen-faced young women, who pinched each other and giggled all the time, putting everybody else out, and causing the Rev. Jenkins at last to beat time with a somewhat elephantine foot. With what delight the good man kept on a long-sustained bass note till he was almost purple in the face! And then came his colleague piping in the treble, "dreaming the happy hours, dreaming the happy hours away."

How happy they were in their own music, these good people, and how delightfully the Vicar beat time gently with one hand on the palm of the other! As to Mrs. Devenish and her sister, it is to their credit that they looked deeply interested and becomingly grave, though the final crash (that surely must have awakened the sleeping lady!) being over, the latter murmured a few words to Dr. Dale that evidently tried his gravity not a little.

"Dear me!" said Mrs. Sylvester, all at once diligently focussing her *pince-nez*, "what vision is this? Why, Constantia, my dear, you never told me. I was quite unprepared for anything so charming."

The charming thing was Estelle, all in black, but black that had glancing lights about it, while a bunch of violets nestled at her throat, and its fellow lay daintily on the brim of a little black net hat.

"You did not see her when we went to the Museum," said Mrs. Devenish quietly, with a twinkle in her eyes; "we only saw the mother. The fact is, Ada, I kept this girl as a sort of pleasant surprise for you. I knew you would be a good deal——"

" Quite so," said Mrs. Sylvester, " and your surprise is delicious." Then, turning to Robert Dale, who was already a favourite with her, she said, " Miss Delano is charming."

The Doctor only bowed.

"My surprise is not at an end yet," said the Vicar's wife; and she and the Vicar exchanged a significant and sympathising glance.

Estelle was presented to Mrs. Sylvester, Estelle a little fluttered and all the prettier for a faint flush that rose to her cheek. She seemed to feel quite a comfort in seeing the Doctor standing by, and even took a step or two nearer to his side. But shortly General Gildea and his gentle wife joined the group.

Robert Dale knew that all Riversdale was agog—saw, as it were, with the back of his head that Mrs. Ponsonby-Cobb had almost fallen off her chair in her eagerness to get a good view of what was going on; that Miss

Arabella and Mrs. Smithers were nudging
one another and whispering; and that Mr.
Ellerby Jones had put on an air as of
being gently shocked, for which the Doctor
would have liked to kick him.

Robert Dale could not stand the ordeal.
Estelle's innocence, the General's ignorance
of the drama that was going on around him,
Lady Gildea's smiling unconsciousness—it was
too horrible.

Estelle—his love, his darling—to be the
sport and pastime of the crowd; the fair
unconscious centre to which all eyes were
turned; and, creeping here and there, as far
too well he knew, foul suggestions and un-
seemly jest!

He made the tour of the garden, greeting
one here, one there; but always avoiding the
spot where Mrs. Cobb was seated with eager
eyes and gaping mouth.

Soon he was conscious of a stir and sensation. People moved about, circling all one
way; and when he turned and looked, there
was Estelle—his Estelle, in spite of any one

and herself too—seated on a low chair just under the shadow of a great cedar-tree, and on her knee a quaint little instrument like a stunted guitar. Then came a delicate tinkling melody, sweet as a bird's warbling, soft as honey—chords of mingled cadence and sweetest rhythm—the opening bars of Offenbach's masterpiece, Belle Nuit.

Yet the sweetest music was yet to come, for a voice, such a voice as he had never heard before, began to accompany the mandoline—a voice that, as the French say, had tears in it, a low, tremulous contralto, rich and deep, and so full of passion and pathos that the man's whole being was stirred to its depths—

> "Belle nuit—O nuit d'amour,
> Souris à nos ivresses;
> Nuit plus douce que le jour,
> O belle nuit d'amour."

What spell was over the girl that she could sing like that?"

Could a woman sing like that, and love be a closed book to her? Estelle had "made a

pastime for herself—a secret pastime for herself—to make the days glad."

And this was her pastime, this——

She had fallen in love.

But not with Robert Dale.

> " O belle nuit d'amour,
>   Ah belle nuit d'amour ;
>   Souris à nos ivresses,
>   Belle nuit, belle nuit d'amour ! "

END OF VOL. II.

*Printed by* BALLANTYNE, HANSON & CO
*Edinburgh and London*

www.ingramcontent.com/pod-product-compliance
Lightning Source LLC
Chambersburg PA
CBHW020810060726
47498CB00017B/1386